The Lotus Flower

Shamim Razaq

AuthorHouse™ UK Ltd.
1663 Liberty Drive
Bloomington, IN 47403 USA
www.authorhouse.co.uk
Phone: 0800.197.4150

© 2014 Shamim Razaq. All rights reserved.

No part of this book may be reproduced, stored in a retrieval system, or transmitted by any means without the written permission of the author.

Published by AuthorHouse   06/26/2014

ISBN: 978-1-4969-8246-9 (sc)
ISBN: 978-1-4969-8247-6 (e)

Any people depicted in stock imagery provided by Thinkstock are models, and such images are being used for illustrative purposes only. Certain stock imagery © Thinkstock.

This book is printed on acid-free paper.

Because of the dynamic nature of the Internet, any web addresses or links contained in this book may have changed since publication and may no longer be valid. The views expressed in this work are solely those of the author and do not necessarily reflect the views of the publisher, and the publisher hereby disclaims any responsibility for them.

To my children and their future,
For my mum for directing me,
For my husband and his support.

Contents

My Brand New Book 1
Me and My Work 3
Words 4
Alone at Last 5
Words and Numbers 6
Shadows 8
Thoughts 9
Patterns 10
Small Wonders of Daily Life 11
Human Numbers 12
Wallflower 14
Sweet Hauntings 21
Sons and Daughters 23
Fragmented Families 25
Panic Attacks 26
Melancholy 27
Tears of Pain 28
Pill 29
Early Intervention Service 30
My World 31
A Poetess Grows 35
Binary Opposites 37
Little Angels 39
Little Ibraheem 40
Rainbow Droplets 42
Ibraheem and the Bullies 43
The Earth Splits to Help it Grow 45

The Autistic Child	47
About Ancestor Voices (Poppies, Roses Lotuses too)	52
Child Dissection	55
In a Womans Voice	57
The Olive Woman	59
Olive Wise	62
Allah (swt) Shower Me With your Blessing	63
The Hermit in me	64
Promise of Purity	65
The Ultimate Test	67
One	69
Virgin Mary/Maryam	70
Soliloquy	71
Lets' Read Revelations	73
The Holy Quran and the Dove	76
Bait-Ullah Heritage	78
The Lavender Flame	79
Light in Gale	81
The Marble Floors of Medina	83
Tie Words with Love	84
Equinox of Earthly Beauty	88
Urdu Poetry	91
Subah Ka Lafaz	92
The Morning Word	93
Mere Ghar Mein Ek Udassi Chaye Hai	94
There is a Strange Sadness in My Home	96
Jeena bhi Jihaad hai	98
Living is to Thrive and Struggle in Allah (swt) Way	99
Watan ki Pehchaan Ban kar	100
Being an Identity for my Country	101

Ekh Khamosh Hissa	102
A Quiet Part of Life	104
Lafzoon ka Sahara Le Liya	106
I Took the Support of Words	108
Searching for Sweetness	110
Battle of Mind and Soul	111
Read Aloud	112
The Story of The Ant	113
An Invitation	114
A Woman in The Third World	116
Women Weaving Garb(age)	117
Excuse a Poetess in Salwar Kameez and Dupatta as she Talks about Voices	120
The Peak of Light	121
Descendants of Adam and Eve	124
Sacred Flower—Love is not Enough	125
The Lone Dandelion	128
I Am Walking	130
Walk of Life	132
Nine Eleven	133
Prince of Darkness	135
Every Strip has a Silver Lining – Gaza	138
Parts of Pakistan	140
What is beyond the Sky?	144
The Sun	146
The Sky at Night	147
Sea	148
Every Cloud has a Silver Lining	149
Pacific Ocean	150
Survival	151

Evening colours	152
Small Blue Flowers	153
The Sandcastle	154
Dents in My Book	155
Entwined	156
Garden of Eternal Eden	157
Dare to Dream—To the Growing Ones	158
Paris	160
To Keats	162
Save The Boy Who Cried Alpha Wolf	164
Life in seasons	166
Unbreakable	167
I Still Write Butterfly	168
Phoenix	169
World of Prosody	170
Possibilities of Algorhythm	174
A Spectrum of Altruism in Autobiographical Autism	175

My Brand New Book

Perfect; Delicate; Innocent and Pure,
Detached from the world, and its war,
The soft first page: I stroke my fingers through,
The pages thirst for knowledge, as they
Flicker through the aromatic breeze.

The feint lines are my visual support,
The solid pink margin is straight as a flying crow.
The shiny front cover is seeking reality,
A whispery echo rushes from the page,
And vibrates in my ear, calling.
My second chance, my brand new book.

Shamim Razaq

No pages turned over, free from my burdens
This time there will be no mistakes,
Each sentence will move along and
Each word will shimmer like glass
Blend in the page, and come alive.

As I write many lyrical wisdoms,
This book will give it form, and make it mine,
Every page will be deep and every space filled,
Every chapter will end before the next begins.
My second chance, my brand new book.

Me and My Work

As long as I have the flow
I will carry on writing
As long as I have a word map,
I will carry on expressing,
As long as I have authorship
I will keep on accelerating,
As long as I have the ability
I will carry on writing.

This is soul searching for me to explore;
How best to present my constellation;
How to turn my work into a universal metaphor;
And turn this work into a memorable collection.

I need the help of family and friends;
I need the help of famous legends;
I need the help of my guardian angel;
I need the help of a good book label;
I need the help of my pen and paper;
I need the help of a peacekeeper;
I need the help of the people who understand;
I need the help of the fork on my hand.

Shamim Razaq

Words

When words begin to fade;
When words begin to whisper;
When words begin to take shade;
When words don't sound crisper;

Art begins to conceive;
Art begins to form,
Art begins to perceive,
Art begins to transform.

The colours begin to blend,
The hands begin to direct,
The mind begins to mend
Words and Art begin to connect.

Alone at Last

At last I have my thoughts,
I have myself my pen and paper
At last I can breathe and relax,
They were calling, but I could not hear.

I was lost deep in some evil trance,
What was lost has now been found,
This is the key to my freedom,
Each bit dedicated to my four little angels with sight and sound.

Things are beginning to get clear,
And people want to see,
But something is not complete, nowhere near,
But one day it will be.

Shamim Razaq

Words and Numbers

From the time of birth.

In this world of words and numbers,
I am lost from all its amazing wonders,
We begin by making sounds,
Talking in syllables, feeling astound.

We stem out and begin to move,
My sentences begin to make to sense,
As the world around me grows,
My curiosity is endless.

My sentences began simple,
But now have a mind of their own,
Like endless patterns on a tapestry,
Each bit speaking in rhythm and in tone.

The numbers in my life keep me in shape,
They began with an instrument,
One; two; three, A; B; C
One for you and one for me.

The Lotus Flower

The sums got complex as I grew,
Found myself lost not knowing what to do,
Let them slip away, believing I did right,
But came back to them in better light.

Sat like a shrunken plant without a stem,
But now they know me and I know them,
The world around me carries on growing,
As I understand its magic maths glowing.

Things are beginning to make senses,
And everything around us has meaning,
In a world of words and numbers,
I am still lost from its endless wonders.

Shamim Razaq

Shadows

In the shadow of the dawn,
Some thoughts come by
In trickles and in echoes,
In singles and in clusters and
In shiny bubbles with an act of their own.

Sometimes they come in duplicates,
So I must slow down, but I
Must not give in, as the coming
Day brings transient beats
With melodious memories.

The nights draw in and
The shadows become darker,
But the thoughts are fresh as ever,
Because the clouds still cry,
But the sun also shines.

Thoughts

Thoughts are coming
like,
Rain
drops,
colourful
rainbow drops,
dancing in tune
and in rhythm.
Something is **bursting** and originating inside me,
I'm writing to understand why,
My hands are supporting my head
And I can't sit upright.

The last week has been
A river of endless thoughts,
The words are falling on to my book
Like snowflakes falling on the ground.

My mind is not with me,
But I am with my mind.
Everything I have been through
Has meaning for me today.
There is energy in my arms
And I am beginning to understand why.

Patterns

Patterns on tiles,
Tessellations and mosaic,
Patterns in the mind,
Some modern and some archaic.

Repeated movements of the hand,
Or repeated events of the past,
Shiny and tanned or dull and bland,
Some the same, some with contrast.

Images and words also come in patterns,
With shapes points and lines,
With grammar, analogies and metaphors
So patterns are embedded in our lives.

Patterns in our own behaviour,
Patterns in our daily routines,
Patterns in our character
And all the patterns in between have a point to make -
So make yours!

Small Wonders of Daily Life

Within the small wonders of daily life,
Live many untold sacred and ghostly tales,
Tales from the distant past and tales from a previous life,
All waiting and pining to be told in details.

They all begin with once upon a time,
Some end in a happy ever after,
While others end in with a tragic crime,
Some bring tears, others burst with laughter.

The story began with Adam and Eve,
Then many were written, and shaped our being,
But the ultimate revelation has declared its place,
So write to better our understanding.

Write as if you have never written before,
Write as if the world depends on it,
Write and reach deep into the core,
Write to show you have done your bit.

Shamim Razaq

Human Numbers

If length multiplies width to find area,
You know your potential energy is gravity.
If multiplying both denominators
Gives you the common denominator,
Then the lowest common multiple should be easy to find,
If a^2 plus b^2 plus c^2 equals d^2 then
The mass is determined,
If sampling methods are bias and sparing,
Then some transfer of energy is wasted,
If angles are measured to fit,
Then $y=mx+c$ is a step upwards.

If square numbers are abstract,
Cube numbers are three dimensional,
And triangle differences increase by one dot each time,
If powers multiply the same number,
Many times, then the innovative number is always original,
If fractions and decimals can be converted into percentages
Then human conversion is natural,
If rational and irrational numbers are important,
Because irrationals are never ending and rationals
Are a majority, then terminating decimals are finite.

The Lotus Flower

If surds have irrational square roots,
Then finding the common difference,
In a sequence should be easy.
If maths is an instrumental or relational approach,
Then some questions are closed while others are open.
If imperial conversions have weight,
Then keeping ten toes down should be easy,
If angles round a point equal 360 degrees,
And half of that equals a line – the horizon meets the eye.
If transformations deal with spatial awareness,
Then why are they limited?
If histograms represent data over a period of time,
Spatial intelligence is achieved.
If sampling methods can be bias,
And scatter graphs measure the line of best fit,
Then the connections are minimum,
If moving averages are mainstream to line of best fit,
Then some of us are being marginalised.

If adding the timed ages of your grandparents,
And all family trees,
Then simplifying with the great grand denominator,
Might not be possible because the numerators might be prime.

Shamim Razaq

Wallflower

There was a girl, bright as a pearl,
Had so many dreams, in which she gleams,
When her soul is taken away at night,
Dreams make way and create inner light,
As she walked watched starked stars sensing light,
As if they have known her all her life,
And she stared up to the zealous one,
Believing he has always been there,
She had known Allah (swt) all her life,
Watching him watch over her so true,
Every dark night in her room,
She dreamed of life,
Living in happiness and freedom,
Gaining spiritual wisdom,
Inside the house made of pure white,
With ripples of rainbow warmness,
And a mind grown in divineness,
A place where love was everything,
Waves of white birds radiant red butterflies sing.

Cultures didn't understand this transformation,
As they told her it was nothing but a false temptation,
She longed for black instead came white with a soul saint,
But false barriers were put with vibes of hate,
Little they knew the harm they were doing,
Separating her as she was spiritually growing,
She tried hard to defend her rights,
And live up to her visions and insights,
But her family never understood her,
Told her she was not important, told she never were,
She said I could be better than I am now,
I want to follow the path of religion and bow,
Bow to my lord who created me,
Follow in his path of eternity,
Live life ever so happily,
So when I stand in front of him with loyalty,
I will have no complaints,
Because I followed his book and his saints,
I moved green earth when I was not happy,
And gained a life of spirituality,
But little people understand,
My mission is to offer a helping hand,
In this world that is in diseases,

Shamim Razaq

I want to bring comfort and yellow warm breezes,
My soul is with me,
My dream my life is the one who created me,
I look at the man made world,
And cry for the Allah made world,
That is full of blush and natural beauty,
And peaceful scenery,
As I know it will make the world a better place,
All I need to do is embrace,
The hand that offers me love and laughter,
The prophet hand that has been here and will be hereafter,
I talked to him all my life and all my days,
He came as a vision in my hopeless days,
Changed my world and told me to do justice,
But I am surrounded by classes of prejudice,
In the dark, he thought I could not sense,
The sensor light,
In thinking I do not have any sense,
He tells me to rise and be brave,
Otherwise I'll end up in an early grave,

The Lotus Flower

If only I talked,
And was not taken away into a foreign land,
Where the starry night shone military stars
But they were never mine,
I listened to the night in silence,
Crunching corn between my teeth,
Under the starlit night,
Being moved through cool air,
Touching, turning star night into sunlight,
And a fine starling flies through the sky,
Where stars over shone the night,
I am left startled,
For the one that was mine.
I write to make sense of this,
But deep down I know what it is,
My life was mapped this way with culture disabilities,
I read the holy book,
And understand where I stood,
This test that was going to change my life,
And I felt weak and entered an internal strife,
I cry and rage on my own,
Turning my heart into silver stone,
So I can burn and then one day shine,

Shamim Razaq

Like a diamond with strength so fine,
When death angels descend from blue sky taking me away,
I would have reached the highest point of worship,
I will present myself to Allah and say, 'Yes, your lordship,'
Allah will see my deeds and my diamond heart,
And see that I was devoted as he to his art.
He will give me my rights and my place,
The rights that this world displaced,
Allah is the greatest, the greatest saviour,
One day he will hear my violet prayer,
For that union I wait,
No regrets and no complaints,
I will be wrapped and protected,
With all the knowledge I collected,
I thank my brave mum for directing me,
Without who I am nothing but an outline of a body,
She gives me strength in her motherly ways,
Without any hesitance or any delays,
From her heart I hear echoes that she speaks,
With warmth, courage, orange floral boutiques,
I say, 'Mum, please pray for me,
I want to be the best for eternity,
I want to save the world and shower love,

The Lotus Flower

Please help me, please share your love.'
When I bowed down to Allah's bounty,
I was moved like the boat on a river,
Swaying in liquid tranquillity so silver,
Ripples and the brittle brown sand with water,
Sends forth the boat opening another chapter,
So smooth the water vibes,
Balancing my bipolar eyes,
That he has sent forth to view,
Thoughts that speak the language of beauty and urdu,
A force reflects in my minds eye,
Showering Allah's momentum from the turquoise sky,
Filling me with a colourful rainbow of blood,
Like the flowers gaining colour still in a bud,
But those colours are for others to love and see,
Like a poets poetry,
I'm waiting for some colour, for my share,
I know it's out there,
I'm fighting a battle,
Hoping things will settle,
I want to fall and cry,
Like the way I was use to dealing with worry,
But my faith and fate does not allow me,

Allah (swt) made me strong for this day,
To move away from pain,
The dry cracks in the ground,
Split and move to help growth,
To grow green ground,
And show early signs of heaven,
But diseases are always close by,
Growing with mother nature as it cries,
Pure love in this world is nothing but a prophecy,
Where one suffer millions believe it's a comedy,
That day will come when headstones will be headstrong,
When graves will open as Allah (swt) angels sing sweet birdsong.

Sweet Hauntings

I can visit the seven wonders of the world,
I will not feel at home until I go to my childhood home.

I can visit the magic fairy wonderland,
I will not feel at home until I dream in my bed at home.

I can talk to great teachers and lecturers,
I will not feel at home until I shout and scream in my childhood home.

I can eat the most rich and sensuous food,
It's nothing like eating from my mum's blessed hands.

I can visit churches, gurdwaras', temples and masjids',
I will not feel at home until I set foot in my mum's home.

I can sit on the throne of a huge lavish palace,
I will not feel important until I sit on the small rug in my mum's home.

I can be treated like royal; having the red carpet rolled,
I will not feel at home until I walk on the welcome mat in my mum's home.

Shamim Razaq

I can ring the bell, within seconds; 'You rang my lord?'
I will not feel at home until I have tea after an hour I ordered it.

I can go to any rich glamorous corner of the world,
I will not feel at home until I run through every room in my mum's home.

I can go to a five star hotel in the most romantic place,
I will not feel at home until I stand by the window looking out for stars in my mum's home.

I can go on a cruise around the world, a chance of a lifetime,
I will not feel at home until I sit with the family and go down memory lane.

Sons and Daughters

Allah (swt) blessed me with two daughters,
Precious, little angels from the heavens above,
Blessings have been counted and the result are they,
My days complete. They give me hope for the next day.

Without them, I would not be a woman
Like a tree without its fruit,
My childhood would not have any meaning,
Like words without its book.

A parent is a source of light energy,
For the child to grow and be nurtured,
Duty of the child is to turn towards them,
For enhancing stronger roots.

The sunflower grows taller,
In the heat of the sun and the coolness of water,
In its finest days its duty is towards the sun,
Before the end of its season.

Shamim Razaq

Allah (swt) honoured me with two sons,
Precious, little angels from the heavens above,
Blessings have been counted and the result are they,
My days complete. They give me hope for the next day.

They bring joy and happiness in my life,
I have a moral duty towards them:
To raise them with love and care,
And there ambitious nature makes me strong.

I know my children will be there for me,
In my hour of need.
My sons and daughters
Will fulfill this wish indeed.

Fragmented Families

A thousand nights of screams,
Shadows on the walls, howling,
No thunderclaps,
Just violent slaps,
Locked in my own comfort zone,
Echoes of violent shockwaves, in the night,
In the electric night,
Visions of death, dominate
Visions of innocent childhood dreams
Dark clouds howling,
Calling, falling to the ground like my
Mum, sisters, brothers
A place which we called home,
My family, my global unity,
My world, our world,
A thousand nights of fears and tears,
Within we curled, from the world.

Panic Attacks

The fuel that generates itself with in me,
The fuel that takes over my body and soul,
Causes calamity; cataclysm and catastrophe—
Keeping me locked up and attached to my comfort zone.

Obsessive worries and unwanted thoughts
Cloud and block me in my mind,
There nature is to be unkind,
Keeping me in isolation, paralyzed and far behind.

The strong shockwaves of panic attacks,
With feelings of strange body sensations,
That increase and take me back to flashbacks,
With deep and dense connections.

Melancholy

Melancholy takes you on an emotional drive,
And your insecure soul lives all the greatest fears.
Your mind and heart are not on your side,
And all the pleasure, hope and happiness disappears.
You fear being isolated: you fear being alone
You fear being alienated: you fear being known.

But there is an interior desire,
A desire that is unexpressed.
There is the light of inner hope
A strength of internal beliefs and
A wish to be free, like a bird in a breeze,
Because living and being is the right of humanity.

Shamim Razaq

Tears of Pain

Tears of pain and memories of fear,
Paralyzed with phobias and panic,
Diagnosed with depression so severe,
At the crossroads with feelings so volcanic

Tears of Pain and memories of fear,
Immersed like the waves in the dense sea,
Cannot sense hope: everything appears so unclear
Cannot taste infinity in life,
Like the sea absent from its precious pearl.

Tears of pain and memories of fear,
So lucid that my life they dictate
Anxiety; angst and anguish
A perfect bunch that bursts and perforates.

Pill

I take the pill with a glass of ice like water,
Dominated,
Bounded
By gunpowder like pill,
Exploding inside me like an eruption of Mount Etna,
Day and night the threatening deathly reminder,
Bitter as it begins to crumble like powder
On my tongue as,
It slithers back down to my stomach,
I feel exhausted as if my whole past has been
Swallowed whole in one go,
It has killed my day of dreams.

Tested on the people of lower class
Checking if it reasons the atomic mass,
More important than
People mass, in the civilised world
Where everything is already prey to the net-world
I meant to take the pill to make me better,
Makes me sick of how it was tested,
On other people like you and I,
Who were tablet tested
Yes, tablet tested
Before they were invested.

Shamim Razaq

Early Intervention Service

The day I was directed to the EIS,
Was the day I thought I was doomed
With the universal battle of mind and heart,
I cried, I screamed, I feared and I pained.

Everyone was evil, or was it just in my mind?
Why did I end up this way, was it their fault or mine?
I believed the latter, convinced my life was about to end.
But that was not enough, the EIS made me comprehend.

I was given a new life, like a withered plant put in the light,
I learnt to keep my self balanced, and hard times at bay,
With lessons on CBT, I know I have come a long way,
This was a walk of life I took, which was reality all the way.

When I was discharged,
I believed the anxieties are going to return,
But when I took that step, breathed passed and beyond a day,
I realised they made me strong for the coming days.

I had a tiny relapse,
But the support I received was encouraging,
With a small dose, love and time,
I feel well and life is worth living.

My World

The silky touch of life slips
Away like mercury with time
My time is occupied
My time is precious
To nurture beauty of my life,
My love for my family
Gets warped in the words of
My tongue,
I hope to go back to them,
To them I return
My intelligent eyes
Seeks reasoning of the human world
And to my emotions I turn
To find the answers
To find understanding
In this metamorphic world
My inner world becomes metamorphic,
As my intellect irons the creases out,
Who can I turn to,
To paint my world out
But myself.

Shamim Razaq

This world I'm living in is different to many
As yarn gets whipped with the wind,
My troubles are with me,
Like harm in a charm,
If only there was ease in a disease,
Then I would not be so deep
In this prophecy,
As my writing was meant to be prophylactic,
My pen works hard
To spell my life out and share many,
To share a world of love and beauty.
My pen remains dominant or is it myself,
That can't see my world detached
From it. Is there life without
Expression?
Is there a tree without leaves?
Is there a world without movement?

The ground below is to dig,
Into and grow courage,
To bloom and to reward yourself
The status of a rose.

The Lotus Flower

Many gardens I have dug,
And now take the courage,
To welcome people, to enjoy to live
A thought and to leave a thought behind
For me to reflect on and add to my garden .
The door is open wide,
Welcoming people
From the rich northern lights—
To all the people from a sacred place.
People from the metal world,
People from the material world,
And people from broken lands,
Reaching all the people from the sphere,
To add what they can,
So I can understand what I think.

Shamim Razaq

I think sitting I'm in a far away land,
Only to find myself
With my family near the electric heat,
In half darkness, and innocent eyes
Their world is made of curiosity,
They look in my eyes and then ask me
To brighten their world
With foods galore,
A smile draws upon my face,
Feeling the life and its reality.
I fear my brain has thrown a bomb,
But I am trying to re establish
Growth, love and beauty.
In the half moon luminous metallic night
The poetess in me awakes
Asks me to write
And add more rhythm to my poetry,
And to dance to the beats of the heart.

A Poetess Grows

Violet aubergines, olive like blueberries,
Shell like moist fruitful treasure,
Producing chemicals of goodness,
To nourish the soul, to expand life,
To bring beauty on thy face,
To eliminate spells, prophecies and charms,
As do creatures in natures care,
Tweet and hunt for these drops of life,
The birds, the squirrels
Treasure nuts in the earth below-
With almonds, walnuts and cashew nuts.

My family tree is full of nuts,
All stored away,
They have to make their way,
The fruits of my womb,
The apple seed and the wheat,
The cracks in the ground.

And the sacred maturing honey
Satisfies the bees in the long summer months,
The squirrels come out,
In the winter for their reward,
As I sit here and write in early spring,

Shamim Razaq

Waiting for rebirth of natures life,
The people of the book,
Tasted the goodness and
Celebrated life with all its joys
And expanded goodness like
The wild flowering plant wishing
To spring to bring the maturity of summer.
If only I had understood oppressions of life,
When I was young,
If only I healed and talked about the wounds of the heart,
I would not be so alone as a peahen
Whose eyes fill with tears when she looks at her feet.

My life gets stuck in my gut,
And my thoughts stop breathing
As I sense death,
But the reverse act of breath
Brings me closer to Allah,
And putting my head level to the ground,
Brings me back to the simplicity of life.

Binary Opposites

If I didn't hide in the dark when I was small,
I wouldn't know what being in the light is today.
If I didn't shout, scream cry and howl
I wouldn't know how to laugh today.

If I didn't feel insecure when I was small,
I wouldn't know what security is today.
If I wasn't thrown in the deep end when I was small,
I wouldn't know how to rise from a fall.

If I didn't rebel against everything when I was small,
I wouldn't know how to accept everything today.
If I didn't understand what mother means when I was small,
I wouldn't know how to be a mother today.

Shamim Razaq

If I didn't get angry with everyone when I was small,
I wouldn't know how to be calm with everyone today.
If I didn't spend all that time alone—wanting to be alone,
I wouldn't know how to want to be with people today.

If I didn't get the education I wanted when I was small,
I wouldn't know how to educate myself today.
If I didn't get the stability when I was small,
I wouldn't know what stability is today.

If I didn't read books when I was small
I wouldn't know how to write today.
If I didn't grow up the way I did,
I wouldn't know who I am today.

Little Angels

Shooting colours and flickering wings
Sparkly eyes and sweet little sayings,
Sometimes dancing, sometimes marching,
In front of my eyes.

Real smiles and innocent thoughts,
Sit in front of me with a wish and a hope,
Their magical playtimes, to me they devote,
To earn a small but fulfilling reward.

'Is it true a tree was a seed?'
Ask tiny beings with innocent smiles.
'How do you do that? I want to know,'
And I want to be like you, when I grow.'

But some little one catches the disease,
Has no magical playtimes,
Or no questions of personal growth,
Life or of oath.

Already lost in the infra red womb,
He tosses and turns with weak time,
Swims deeply into the sweet scent,
Only to be lost in the nucleus of darkness.

Shamim Razaq

Little Ibraheem

There was a dream when I said no,
No to the baby who was not born,
The baby who cried more food with woe,
The answer was no: What will I feed my daughters?
So the baby did not born.

He came in my dream as a vision,
Not understanding the signal,
I was fearful without any other provision,
Lost and decayed he then became fictional.
I could not save him.

The occasion lived slow and motionless,
There was pain in the small red room,
There was nothing but darkness
In the room of my womb.

The wind wailed, the clouds came closer
The sun burnt and the willows waned,
The glass cracked and things got worse,
Colours darkened and the ghosts laughed.

The Lotus Flower

But years went by and along came the chosen one,
Found some happiness and loved him with all my love,
But the baby that was lost was still lost
Accepted, moved on but still missed the above.

One day, without telling anyone he came back,
This is the baby, that I lost I am sure this is that baby,
I feel him grow-crying and laughing I am taken aback,
I had moved on but nature knows best .
Felt contented every time he moved and kicked,
Protected myself for him from medication and harm,
This is the baby that I had lost, this is how he looks like,
Round shiny eyes; the cutest of them all.

I was right. He was born and I looked at him.
See, I was right this is the one I lost,
All those years ago, we named him Ibraheem
With angelic looks he came at no extra cost.

But the ghosts came attacking and laughing,
Protected him and my children from evil beings,
Now he is growing, the dream was he, yes he,
The little angel came at the right time to save me.

Shamim Razaq

Rainbow Droplets

He looks for the love from the corners of his droplet eyes,
He turns around and turns around again,
To capture the moment as many times,
But now he has to pass the moment .

At school time he looks out for me,
From the hustling and bustling crowd,
He lights up when he sees me
Eager: to tell me the good work and make me feel proud.

He walks holding onto his baby brothers' pushchair,
And fighting against the cold chilling wind,
He begins to talk with waving hands in the air,
He hangs his belongings on my arm-that's his daily discipline.

'That's your Baby brother and this is mine,'
Says his friend pulling at his coat,
'I was Star of the Day and I got a sticker.'
'So, I have my mum and my baby brother.'

'Mum what's for tea? I am hungry.'
'It's a surprise, you just wait and see.'
So he walks on, and then runs to the car,
Still looking from the corner of his rainbow droplet eyes
Catching the love from my eyes.

Ibraheem and the Bullies

Ibraheem was an intelligent boy,
He went to school with joy,
He read all his sums right,
His teachers said he was very bright.
One day, he was picked on and teased
So he told his teacher and felt eased.
The teacher told them off,
But the bullies began to scoff,
A few days later he was pushed and shoved
His fear increased as he felt unloved,
He tried and tried to stay strong,
He cried and cried when all his sums read wrong,
He didn't know what to do anymore,
Because playtimes seemed like a never ending war,
Soon, he lost all his friends,
Every corner became dead ends.

Shamim Razaq

The weather was wintry cold,
Slowly his dilemma began to unfold,
His parents found out he was far behind,
He told how the bullies were unkind,
He faced his problems and felt better,
The bullies felt very bad
For making Ibraheem feel very sad,
They apologised and felt ashamed,
They bullied him, they claimed.
They felt much worse than Ibraheem had,
Which was *really* very sad,
That was there last time,
They promised to be kind,
So slowly they changed,
With Ibraheem friends they became,
They live to tell their story,
Making sure it stays in his(story).

The Earth Splits to Help it Grow

Personalities are divided when parents are divided,
And the clash within the child arises,
The depths of emotions rupture leaving the child unguided,
And depriving the child from growing in confidence,

If there was love and union in the hearts,
When they first tied the knot,
Then there would not have been many split ends,
If only they gave it one true shot.

The war within splits, and ends refuse to meet,
With so many dilemmas, everything remains in shattered bits.
Sometimes things resolve, other times they go on hold,
Why do I find myself in this recurring fear?

A fear that is dark, unseen, and unheard,
I sit down and write down my feelings in words.
When the atmospheric tides clash causing storms and depression,
I understand this nature and continue in writing and communication.

You see many fall in love shortly after marriage,
Then it dies leaving an unbalanced bank of emotions,
The battle begins with: 'not I, but you,'
Saying this, they split apart and enter many confusions.

Then comes the battle of the social classes,
One says I come from a very privileged family,
The other says I am no less, my father was great in his time,
What hoodwink! They come from the same family line.
A split society splits the human mind,
Then it is labelled an illness and people are withdrawn,
Why are there so many divisions,
When we all share the same smile and sentiments?

A split personality is nothing but a beautiful growth,
Because the world has to split to help it grow,
By splitting words we understand them better,
Humanity should stay close to nature,
If they really want to understand human nature.

They ramble on leaving the child by the window,
With fireworks exploding inside and out,
The ghostly, grey smoke glides through the sky,
And the popcorn fireworks burst far above the ground,
Dropping transient twinkles in the twilight.

But the child by the window will always be there,
No matter what the time or season,
Sometimes the child will understand,
Other times it will be hard to reason.

The Autistic Child

The possibilities mother nature grows
In the natural world with all fairness,
Is living the happiest highest standards
Of heightened starry awareness,
With gramophone like ear drums,
Bulbous 3D eyes echo locating church visions,
As bats play the night magnetic field:
Butterflies; cricket; marching ants and spittle bugs,
Reflective studs umbrella like wings with insight
Religious bead like eyes draw in the prey,
With zooming night shades of winged colours
The church bats know how to prey,
The silent owl flight
And the iridescence feathers of blackbird mystics,
Ascends to higher levels of spiritual growth
With detached retina water images,
The peacock feathers,
The spectrum of autumn colours the warm yellow eyes glow,
Healing the face mask of communication
With a fascination of words and numbers,
Spirituality saved by the five k's spiritual teacher—Gobind Singh—
The autistic child comes out to play bookworm—
The blind mans' walking stick,
The domestic silverfish and the whitefly,

Shamim Razaq

Anything is possible –
With winter icicles freezing spring flower pink bulbs in China,
Dark circles—missing spark—the ability to label my own disability
Makes words fly of the page.
Seeing only the white page and spiritual words
I thank Allah (swt) for holy congregations.

Lacking social communication
Magnetises me to the salah of communication,
Where thick degree border lines are challenged –
My balance is restored by images of Ka'ba,
My beating impulse Islamic nature stops
The impulsive devil from socially isolating me,
As whispers hold absorb black spectrum death –
Osmosis rainbow spectrum remains speechless,
As wavelengths are echoed into colourful sound bites and opalescence ripples,

The Lotus Flower

My thoughts are preternatural as my senses are heightened.
The rainbow red, orange fruit, yellow emotions,
The basic needs for motivating survival,
The balancing chrome green with visions of blue, indigo, violet
Intuitional idealism cubed intellectual creative imagination,
The seeds the bat craves carves
Them into the forest where the sweet berries grow,
Reshuffling the magnetic nervous system,
The electrifying rainbow light shines indigo,
The autobiographical colours of autism
Sends forth a water light heat spectrum,
As I am reminded of the holy Quran
Interpreted by Muhammad (pbuh),
As he read goodness that was spread
Across complex eventful words in concave communication,
Where the iridescence silk white rope of the spiders web
Saved his insights and sacred visions,
As Allah (swt) promised humanity in the most simplest of simplest fashion.

The longest wavelength of physical red attraction,
Ignites clear blueprint of trusted intellectual acquisitive communication,
With pillar like tall sunflower characteristics
The bees dance acrostic green balance,
Indigo intuitional violet idealism matures—
Centuries old golden healing heals the creative imagination.
Where Darwin studied past physical behaviours
Giving huemans characteristics of apes,
Motivated Lemark to study linguistic behaviour
Acquisition defining changes in a giraffes neck!
If only mortals metaphorically connected
The past with the present future,
They would understand animals are a metaphor for hueman behaviour,
When immortals Adam and Eve repented –
They portrayed a hueman act,
Leading to centuries of rosemary prayers,

And salah miracles for mortals to recondition and interact,
In languages of earthly land the tongue speaks many restored rhythms,
From body, sign language and spoken words
Languages have come a long way,
To re-establish culture, hueman[1] hereditary and intellectual awareness,
The possibilities mother nature grows,
In the natural world with all fairness,
Living the happiest, highest standards,
Of the heightened starry awareness for future words play.

---

[1] This was done deliberately to express the different shades of human and life.

Shamim Razaq

About Ancestor Voices (Poppies, Roses Lotuses too)

Look. Dekko.[2]
From one voice, from the back of my mind,
Voices with tones and notes,
From a distant past, echoes
repeating echoes,
I told them to stop it, to stop being bad,
To stop making me bad,
They haunted me,
I am sensitive, i am easily affected,
I fight for little pleasures in my daily mind,
I fight back. My face has lost its pride,
Not egoistic pride,
A pride of security
That every soul is born with
Its rock hard to fight it,
To fight demons,
The battles of the introvert extrovert world
To fight within yourself,
And then to come out rock hard,
My vision is refracted before its reflects
In my tear sac,

---

[2] Urdu term for look

My mind is split before it connects,
(Then sadly labelled schizophrenic,)
But I was connecting and linking,
Because I fought a battle for peace and love,
The creases on my face,
The battlefield within and,
The ruptures, tortures and
The wounded battle fields were deserted
Then,
The poppy with four to six petals came.

And,
Our gardens are a garland of soft roses;
Growing within the thorns and with full of emotions—
In the crumbled soil below.
The lakes are laid with the lotus,
As they have fought from the depths of the waters,
Carrying hope, light and purity in their shield like petals.

Shamim Razaq

Which do you resemble, Rose, Poppy or the Lotus?

The battles of the earth
Have left deep cuts
And lasting bruises on the land.
Look. Dekko.
The land is fighting its own
volcanoes and tsunamis,
cracks, underwater plate clashes and rising sea levels,
It does not have a flight option,
It has to fight to let beauty grow on the landscape.
Look . Dekko.

Child Dissection

The children of the Aztec world—killed
So that evil lead leaders could get compensation
From God if they give him the price of a life,
This artificial religion still lives today,
Like artificial flavours,
No wonder children have nightmares,
Punished by cactus spines and toxic chilli smoke,
This is child bondage without the bandage at its best,
From the north, east south and west,

In the civilised world child classification
Prospers in schools and institutions,
Children are pressured to grow brain,
Look but don't see,
Bring power back in the country,
Advertisements tell them,
They have to have the latest gadget,
To stay in the violent game.

Shamim Razaq

In Asia girls shaped to stay at home,
Told to weave, to prick their dreams out,
On a tapestry—told not to look beyond the perimeters,
Or speak out of tune but to talk to shadows
And burn in them and not utter a word.

To children abused and tormented in chambers,
Females circumcised fired with acid, beaten and assaulted,
As they walk like militants in their country,
What a circus ride of humans walking the planet!

In a Womans Voice

In a womans voice a child came out,
She speaks her heart as lips pout,
She remained quiet for so long,
For twenty years she stayed strong,
She put up with violence,
She lived in oppressive silence,
She brought up her kids with a hope,
Didn't tell anyone she couldn't cope,
She lived on little and relied on God,
In her own little quad,
She suffered on her own,
If only she had known,
There was help outside,
She would not have cried and cried,
She did want to put the familys honour at stake,
So she continued alone in agony, pains and ache,
Her kids grew and parted ways,
As she stood all alone as always,
She didn't mix in with the world,
And within she curled,
One day she had had enough,
She told her daughter she had enough,
The daughter understood,
As she heard the child cry about her livelihood,
In front of her was her mother,
And no one other,
She listened to the childhood voice

Shamim Razaq

Without any choice,
She felt bad for not understanding her mother,
But now she promised she will bother,
The mother continues to let her childhood out
To help her understand what childhood is all about,
She had tough times with her spouse,
But now all the problems are coming out,
It is hard to accept the life ahead,
But everything has been said,
She shares wise words with people she knows,
Leaving a beautiful fragrant of a rose,
She takes each day as it comes,
Feeling better rather than numb,
She lives for God night and day
As she continues to pray,
But there is a child like voice still inside,
Which she still at times tries to hide,
Her life has been wasted away she says,
As she talks about the past days,
Her daughter consoles,
The mother talks about the evil souls,
Finding it hard to let go,
As they have drilled deep inside,
Leaving her vulnerable and brushed aside.
In a woman's voice a child came out.

The Olive Woman

The multiple synapse reacts to isolation,
The syntax of my words finding their lost way in my wordbook,
As symptoms altered to suit the manmade world –
Where is me?
The one who dared to dream big with big ideas,
In this small world,
I struggle to find loves voice.

The symbolism of the nightingale
Or the flicker of the lavender flame – absent
From my soul – the aviary of my soul
Word searches the missing link
Between sentimental veins and the logic of my mind,
Juggling my jugular veins to reason my mind,
The mother cried her loudest yet,
With breaths of panic attacks,
Her orbiting hands round her sons head,
Cried for people for not understanding the powerful psyche mind,
The broken homes, shattered bonds,
The shaking of the souls core,
With refracted eyes and the stigma of madness,
Begins reasoning with
The centuries old outer world war,
The battles of the hearts,
The reasoning of the minds,

Shamim Razaq

Sometimes it's hard to justify,
So she wanders through lifes' tragicomedy.
And, one day spiritually she walked the green turf,
Dropping tea leaves through olive fingers,
With beaten frame distorted mind,
The summer spring dawned on the dome of the olive tree,
With twig spirals and leaves green,
The lavender rose light bud flickers,
In early morning heat,
The dove flight in starry skies,
Vibrant wings and bowed heads,
Reflecting justice scales that are timed,
The Quranic verses recited Allahs (swt) almighty name,
Clashes unchained,
The freedom of the words,
Have done much to change,
The backlashes of society,
She cries: 'My prophets name is being abused.'
Her lethargic unlettered words,
Begins to reason peoples psyche,
Turning ants into daylight ashes,
Giving up on mortal life,
The phoenix rhythm – temporary time temporary pain,
Restores heavens eternal delight,

The Lotus Flower

With visions of love and dreams of life,
The heart does not lie,
The dark human sun based shadow
With the dark side of the glowing moon
Mysterious thoughts bright early spring glooms,
Shows life is in the making,
The temporary soul changes into an angelic spirit,
As she talked about the Iraq war,
Blaming herself for the diseases of family traditions
Still –
Seeing light in the darkness of society
The charcoal colours the visions drawn,
The vibrating echolocating waving moon,
The clashing oceans, with inner darkness,
Wide eyed ready for flight,
I lie down in the darkness of night,
Waiting for what?
I wish I knew.

Shamim Razaq

Olive Wise

She sat with layers of years behind her with psyche power,
With olive wise Nur[3] lit eyes and crescent vision,
In front of the geometrical hexagonal chemistry flower,
She tells me to do justice and adapt to human nature,
I see deprived children, famished third world families,
She reminds me of being grateful—to thank the creator,
Whom she worships everyday with cultural responsibilities,
Away from cursed love and black magic macabre,
She brings me home with warmth and care,
Sealing my wounded heart,
She reminds me of the blessed olive woman with gold hair,
Who cried: 'My prophets name is being abused.'
With strong feminine demeanour, she plays Mother Teresa,
With visions of freedom with peace of angelic doves,
Descending from heightened celestial electrical magnetism,
From heights beyond the sky to the land of education.

---

[3] Urdu term for light

Allah (swt) Shower Me With your Blessing

The tasbeeh between my fingers,
Each stone orbits vibes within me,
I sit here and reflect spiritually,
With feelings of religious unity,
Breathing positive opportunity,
For the future with my poetry,
Every stroke and every flick is my remedy,
Circle of life, this is my reality,

If clouds could cry loud,
Then I want to be part of that beauty,
Allah (swt) send me down rain,
Allah (swt) fulfill this necessity,
It is a blessing shower me this hospitality,
I thank Allah (swt) for this insight and immortality.

Shamim Razaq

The Hermit in me

The hermit in me rises from prostration,
After the salah of communication;
My mind focussed on purification;
My day will flourish in liberation.

My senses are enlightened;
I sense pearl moments of peace—brightened;
Which I treasure deep inside,
As I finish my salah in modest pride.

My spiritual self has been restored,
And I prey for goodness from my lord.
The colours rich and tiniest and tiniest of things I see
From an angel like spirit dispersing in natures care,
And vapour like sacred drops absorbing in the air

The softness and serenity is in natures scenery,
As I feel cherished in the warmness around me,
Soft percussions of the verses I have read circulate in the air,
Tapping and touching something inside me.

Rich rose aromas of natures products boost in sensitivity,
As sweet aubergines and cucumbers burst in productivity,
With great gusto the metamorphic food grows
As my soul rises in light prosperity.

Promise of Purity

People come in colours,
and layers like the rainbow,
As one end goes up,
Reaching the heights of life,
While the other end treasures down.

The pure rainbow droplets that fall before,
Brings light into our eyes,
As we witness the colourful pearl drops,
Reflecting and refracting
In the ambience of atmosphere.

True is he to his creation,
Creating unity amongst his people,
And wishing them good,
And we live to retell the story,
As a miracle.

Shamim Razaq

The paper boat, the water,
Or the adult, whose depressing,
Feelings of inner Hypothermia,
Drifts away with the boat,
In the distance, on a calm river,
For us to see,
Reflections in the rainbow arc,
Droplets come direct from heaven, to utilise,
To give seedlings the best spring of life,
And replenish the earth with nourished beauty.

The Ultimate Test

The culture clash and the ultimate test,
Has left me feeling humble,
Labour and logic in this world will mean love in the next,
And we are born as kings and queens
But we have to die as faithful slaves,
Logic says some of us flourish in our prime,
And life says we die as slaves,
While others are here to live
and dwell in earthly matters, I am here to translate and narrate .
Our names carry an authentic meaning,
And with time this gives the world a meaning,
If forget—me—nots could remind people of their presence,
Why can't me?

Allah creates with logic,
And gave you creativity in the form of your name,
If only Allah gave names then logic would,
Make sense to the people who think what's in a name,
If emotions are born with us then why are they to blame,
If only we could accept life death and all the binaries,
If only we could understand the reason Adam and Eve came,
Then we would spiritualise for the eternal fame.

Shamim Razaq

My past was my beginning,
And my present will be my future,
My death in this world will mean life in the hereafter,
We are told to love to a level of loyalty,
And then destroy our right to love,
We are taught to humiliate till hate,
What a great test i am under,
What great power lies behind this natural force,
Can humanity accept lovers of life,
In bodies that have been deserted?

Love comes in many forms,
Why are some denied and some accepted?
And still we are tested to love,
Our hearts are tested and no wonder women die of cancer!
My tears are dry,
And my heart struck a thunderstorm,
My every salah purified me,
Like the commas in my poetry.

One

All prophets came with the same message,
In their times of trial to save humanity from harm,
Each nation, each timeline is sitting their own trial,
So why deny one when we should unite as one.
Under the native sun let ourselves grow,
For the knowledge of then and now,
We all stand a trial join me if you want – now,
To show love is always around,
When the world is in bounds,
Love has to stand, defend and make grounds,
To bring life back in the souls that are culture bound
By false traditions, values, beliefs and attitudes,
Show them the light of love and hope,
That never could bury the reality rope,
Show them the insight of the telescope,
And let them look at patterns,
And the connections like the inside of a kaleidoscope.

Shamim Razaq

Virgin Mary/Maryam

My fears will always be part of my poetry,
Hidden somewhere in the corner of my voice,
A fear of suffocation and
Archaic patterns, that clash with inner wars,
And labels attached that don't have any meaning.

I think and wonder how virgin Mary grew,
With battles and brutality of her true identity,
She held onto the spiritual rope of her reality,
And produced the best amongst her nation,
He spread the truth with clear affirmation.

What spiritual time was born named Christianity
That bought order and justice to humanity,
It was a time of self discovery,
That promised the nation another prophet shall come,
With the heartbeat of the final drum.

Soliloquy

Had I not feared and had I not dried my tears,
I wouldn't be sitting here with contradistinctions,
In my mind that has captured a world of rhythm,
Blending in many creeds and writing a soliloquy,
As I pay homage to all thoughts of the human heart and brain,
That have gathered stones for the memorial of spiritual reign,
In this crossed world, I sit and write a crossword,
For people to see the world as one brain,
And all languages follow the same food chain.

Can we then deny the fact there was one Adam and Eve
Who we all descend from, and one Creator,
Who is the best facilitator and protector?
In our minds and hearts, who we worship openly and secretly,
In a private or public congregation, what is the difference,
When beliefs are one?
Why the chronic illness
When we all share the same chronicles?

In his creation,
There are cymbals that vibrate many tales,
Had I understood this world earlier,
My world would have been different,
We would be a couple but who is an ocean away,

Shamim Razaq

I hold onto evergreen emerald and violet visions,
I'll be waiting at the seraglio as your seraph,
Wrapped and protected like the sepals,
Which protect the petals of the lotus,
In this prescriptive world,
I write out my own prescription as a couplet:
The four chambers of the human heart,
The centre of all creativity and art.

I write to eliminate discriminations,
But who knows what creeds breed in the world of cultures,
Cultures never understood dreams,
Ignite the light of love and hope
See where insights will take me.

In this world of webbed contradictions,
I write lines to eliminate diseases from my world.
The tag of scars, have healed my arm with the pain it caused,
I'm left with reflections from the past to grow from,
To move on in the world map,
To tell no matter what I was here and I survived,
And I lived, I lost, I gained, I lived again,
I paid a price and I made my point.

Lets' Read Revelations

Heart homelands broken, languages of our zameen[4] stolen,
Adams pious voice protests ignorant transgressors and prophetic blasphemous,
Where our very emotional essence in being is in turmoil and challenged,
People protest placards with revenge in solid chests damaged,
In hostile lands and death smoke blinding sunlight intelligence,
Bruised hearts and minds defend their apple of the eyes perseverance,
Dekko even the bruised fruit carries seeds for potential and growth,
Hoping to return to its mother natures womb for regrowth.

Even the stonehearted moved and sang out tears from the heart,
As Allah speaks to his people lives through mother natures nurtured art,
The deep season of September change shows its everlasting effects,
Winter will bring still white death to earth so spring can reconnect,
To the *walis*[5] of Allah sighting daily salah to expand life and recollect,
To enhance and proclaim prophet Muhammad (pbuh) is our saviour,
From the very first revelation of Mount Hira,
Our prophet read the words of Almighty Allah.

Like iridescence light sound squeezed through coloured leaves of emotion,

---

[4] Land
[5] Friend of Allah

Like opalescence captured coloured water rainbow with inner diffracted light oceans,
As I perform salah, decrease wrinkles and see this unique captured sight.
How I pray to Allah to show people this perpetual light,
That will grow intelligence and educate the mind and heart,
That will help people with soul, sound, sight and art,
To live their full potential and reflect wholly onto future generations,
So Islam can see a change for children in the next generation.

For children to grow their best potential in Allah (swt) abundant light,
To help purify souls and land to grow earth like Adam (AS) with his first fight,
Our prophets' insights shook all earths diamond colourful volumes shaking the core,
Bringing it to the surface with intrinsic ethics and distinctions,
So much is possible from mother natures greatest book of recitations,
That we live, learn, grow and eat its fruit from with moments of congregations,
Open your heavenly minds and enrich it with goodness that was spread,
Tell people who we are in this world that continues to be misread.

Seeds returning to the ground, promise potential for generations to come,
To live the beauty, reflect and learn from its maturing season,
To show the spirit of life again, again and again,
Why does humanity repel living tomorrow instead living in the spirit that was then?

Shamim Razaq

The Holy Quran and the Dove

Open—like the Holy Quran –
The Great Muslim guidance book,
Like wings of dove,
No veil yet a veil of assured concealed faith
Between Allah (swt) and I when I recite,
And no veil yet a veil between angels grip.

When poverty stricken people show sincerity to Allah,
Their prayers are heard yes their prayers are heard.
Like no veil between a slave writing a words book,
Austere complexion trailing across water space,
With angelic watermark and your snowdrop body,
Holds answers to high held heaven in form of coloured light,
The snow wind captured words as the dove cuts through,
And the wind captured love settles into my writing book,
The snow hill mountains underneath the rivers flow,
As violet flower daisies look upon the show,
When scattered birds bones come to life at Allahs' call,
And darkness turns into positive light,
My words are polished onto my page,
To articulate like never before.

The winter white freeze turns over to an empty page,
Settles down to welcome more words,
Like specks of freshly scattered snow illuminating crystal clear,
Articulating beyond human norms like never before,
No devil motivated, evil lived eyed or no magic macabre,
Nor the ego-centric or the worldly beings
Can stop my praise for Allah (swt),
As I thank him the life he has
Given all.

Bait-Ullah Heritage

Deforming the spiritual lighting growth,
Will inherit a heart of Bait-ullah heritage of Phoenix glowbal living,
For future space time reviving literatures intergrowth,
Diffusing streams of burnouts by voltage force into floral rich leaves,
As Almighty Allah turned dead bones into knowledge pledged birds,
That were scattered on high hills in spiritual times of rich colour,
To revelate word stems of acquired knowledge of honour for earth based planet,
For future centuries purifying heart disease with centuries old pomegranate,
The riches of language and the poor slaves of Almighty Allah,
Will find reconnection in times of terror Ma' sha Allah, Sub' han Allah,
As Muslims attract to Bait'ullah and Allah (swt) focussed Qibla.

The Lavender Flame

The vibrations of Allah's call
Vibrates the coloured leaves,
As the candle flickers,
Fluttering my eyes in mid afternoon,
During my midmost prayer
Focussed on Allah (swt) hub light of clarity,
My heart recites to see,
His abundant light waves of love,
For his children,
In this world that holds
Broken hearts and broken dreams
Of his children,
Artificial pill bounded
By labelled grim age
As circulation in the ka'ba represents
Eternal spiritual growth
Reuniting for eternal age of
Paradise in the six sided cube
For life to flourish we must die.

Shamiin Razaq

My rushing river of tears
Fail to burn out the Nur of my candle,
That devil inflicted whispers blow,
In'sha Allah the Nur will light,
The world with its wisdom,
With angel gripped soul,
Lavender scented, carved pillar like
Lighting with the reality rope
Of coloured wax –
Ornament of the purified home,
The winter berry, the river of tears,
The melting flakes
Or the diffracted light in the river.
The candle continues to glow on
The melted wax as the rope of reality
Keeps it alive,
Like a paper boat on a river,
The lavender flame.

Light in Gale

My notion protected by a violet calyx,
Learnt the lesson of love by breaking my own heart,
Learnt to sing among crops of diverse flavours,
Cloistered with Allah (swt) wisdom of light,
Transformed for a while,
Into a changeling,
Contemplating times when the peace of heavens,
Reflects on fajr time,
The green gardens of village life,
The sizzling rain.

Solitude.

In the distance, a potters clay
Hardens in the fire,
As I am forced to burn daily but true to my nature,
I become a strong soul fighting devils daily,
The grey clouds,
The thunderstorm,
The lightening of my ancestors land
Is calling me to grow,
The innocent candle sheds her warmth
Without being touched,
Growing daily visions to help my ancestral land grow,
To implement, to compliment

Shamim Razaq

My heartfelt part of potassium flame globe,
Moulded is my heart with Almighty Allah (swt) light,
And yet I am reminded the reasons I broke it,
My tears trickling daily searching Mother Mecca,
As my daily salah turns to the first house of almighty Allah,
To find security in this unsecure world,
The sky scraping illuminating night light
Reflects on the sacred paths,
Calling my people to purify, bow and prostrate,
To grow the same light in your diseased land,
Which is negatively charged and sprayed with ions of disease—

The war struck women,
The abandoned children,
The innate soil bleeds its innermost cries,
As women warble woe to warhead,
Make stem cells headway strong
Make osmosis possible –
Turn corrupt erupted soil into a birdsong,
So our children can look up proud
At the watermark of Almighty Allah (swt) love,
Make mutation beneficial transporting
Blood transpirations
To the sacred chambers of the heart,
Planting flow of energy to every part of nature.

The Marble Floors of Medina

THE Marble floors of Medina,
The mesmerising sky,
The sacred paths,
And the stories of people told,
The illuminating olive light,
The masjid of salah[6],
Blessing walks of life,
Building strong narrative arcs,
The tears of pain,
The laughter of eternity,
The visions of Muhammad (pbuh)
The way to Allah (swt).

---

[6] Prayer

Shamim Razaq

Tie Words with Love

The muneer[7] of the sun casts
Clouds of moonlight,
On the shadow of the earth,
The moisturising illuminous oil
Of the African Olive divine tree
Beacons the night sky,
The illuminating rock like rose
The hologram – idyll,
Like moonflower glowing with locus nectar,
The oceans of storms purified,
The crescent time of Islam,
Floating with serenity and tranquillity,
Reflective dazzles dissolving in the distant fertile sea,
Watching the backdrop as nature mends,
My broken heart giving me inner peace and end to an inner war.

Ya'sin[8].

---

[7] light
[8] O' man

The Lotus Flower

The heavy clouds lightened
As whispers tried to blow my words away,
Left humble against devils play,
As Qu'ran radiated light as it continually makes way,
I sit reflecting villages of graveyards,
Still telling myself : Heal thy self,
With the aroma of red rock rose
Spread on top of tombstones,
Where the wind wanes
And voices speak within,
Looking into the locus of the dark night,
Questioning stars about fate,
Pleading to be guided by Allah (swt) guiding eternal light.
The composed nature has turned into
Concave decomposed battles of the world,
Women cremated and combusted,
The hidden breaths in village life with honour wars,
Burying and burning daughters east and west,
Written as an epitaph, claiming epoch energy,
To live once more,
As I see my psyche world crumble in front of me,
I wish to live in a world without prejudice,
Where the warmness of the sun enters skin,
Where play means growth,

Shamim Razaq

In hot summers gold spin,
Where religions blossom with peoples devotion,
Claiming ring of halo energy,
Reclaiming democracy,
To live,
To live once more,
In a world without war,
My devoted love is real that dares to love
and loved be the earth.

She said: 'I didn't choose this life it chose me.'
As my motherland educated me,
The soil, the breeze, the village simplicity,
The blessed hearts of femininity,
Who cherish heartfelt moments,
The starstruck lightning between
Windstruck windows bringing blessed
Light of opportunity, locating me
To live once more
One more time
To visit my motherland,
To reshape it,
Into a dozen endless months,
With a dozen endless full moons

The Lotus Flower

Starlight lovestruck
Of natures rainbow silk ribbon
To purify centuries of emotions
As the height of my heart settles,
The snowflakes fight for the ground – I smile,
I sit and watch the point the earth and sky unite and reunite,
Wrapped with the crescent time of Islam
And the striking stunning stars,
Ornament of the night sky –
Shedding security I made dandelion wishes,
With green leaflets of hope,
For violet, ruby red love to blossom,
In all parts of mother natures cry,
With clusters of white olive flowers,
As stars stun the dark,
And every evening rock rose
Transforms into a blue sky
With radiating, transient beats,
Of the morning arc,
As my motherland mellow,
Inspires me to tie words with love.

Shamim Razaq

Equinox of Earthly Beauty

What absolute equinox of earthly beauty
Wraps human sentimentality,
And thought,
Holding faith growing spring colours of equilibrium,
On this cocooned earth playing and growing the magnetic field,
Into a worshipping mind –
The floating cinder on the river,
The flame on the candle,
The shadows of time on the sundial,
The graceful swan on water,
Carrying courageous smiles absent placebo pills.

To all seasons – I perfect my deen
For the eternal garden
I see blind love –
The truth of our beloved anchor I adhere to,
As he (pbuh) veined white light
In the darkness of society,
Giving the token coinage of Islam to live in peace.
But my auditory nerves causes a genocide stirrup,
And let me tell you something—growth overcomes all diseases
So the earth can grow and flourish.
My nature inspired nature praises Allah (swt) nature.

During the death of day,
My arm arteries bruised, my spine hurt,
Nerves beaten,
Yet I hold my heart in my labelled body,
Wondering is my heart big enough for this world?
And was I ever truly loved?

Still –

The night lights heaven secured stars,
As souls are taken to practice
Early steps to eternal times of heaven,
Early morning we wake up purified and forgiven,
Holding dreams with stars floating beauty,
Taking solar power of solar energy,
Focussing our secured eyes in daily motion,
And ultramarine light like reality rope
Veins pulsing red cells to all parts of humanity,
And round pearl like tasbeeh beads
Cells orbiting both poles of the dome daily.

Shamim Razaq

I sit here, smiling at lifes tragicomedy,
With quran recitations vibrating,
My anchor,
The hermit in me,
Grows daily to depict diamond dreams and du'aas,
Of Almighty Allah(swt) scribed reality,
As I bow down in humble salute to the purist scriber,
Still believing what absolute timed Earthly beauty
Wraps the equinox
Of spring sentimentality and thoughts.

Subhan' Allah.
Alhamdulilah.

Urdu Poetry

28th February 2013 – Few days with Dadda jis visions.

Mein ne apne dada jaan Abdul Rehman koh ekh khwab mein dekha – wohi bhadur ankhen aur chohra seena lagaye huein shaan se betein hain. Hawa ka halka sa ehsas hai. Jo roshni ki taraf goongunatha hain. 'Beti, yahaan dekho, tumhari ankhein kahan hain, tumhari ainak ka sheesha kahan hain, zara pehen keh dekko. Is khwab ke baad yeh lafaz mere kanoon mein goonganaye.'

I saw my grandad in my dream, he was sitting tall and proud with his broad chest and brave eyes. A warm wind is beating and blowing mildly towards the light. 'Daughter look here, where are your eyes, where are your glasses, put them on and then see what happens.' After this dream the following words came to me.

Shamim Razaq

Subah Ka Lafaz

Har subah ka har lafaz
Har zubaan ki awaaz fajr ke roop mein farz doondtha hain,
Har awaz ki ekh pehchaan hain
Jo zameen sajde mein goongunathi hain,
Har lamha, har soch ke chalne wali zubaan apni pehchaan
Haq se mangtha hain.

Kyun khamosh ho? kyun naraaz ho?
Apni maa ki duaaon seh,
Allah subhan a wataala ki niyamat
Se dunya abaad hain – Shukran Allah.

Khuda ka diya –
Dunya ki roshni mein sab se aala hai
Sitaare bhi khuda ki roshni
Ke sadqe mein sadiyon se waqaf hain,
Raat noor se roshan hai,
Aur shaitaan se nijaat pane ke liye hazir hain.
Subhan' Allah, Alhamdulilah.

The Morning Word[9]

Every mornings every word,
In every tongue, in the spirit of dawn
Searches for obligatory words,
Every tongue has its own identity,
In which it sings during prostration of prayer
Every moment, every thoughtful tongue
Rightly asks for its true identity.

Why are you quiet
And away from your mums blessings?
With the blessings of Allah the world is living
Thankyou Allah (swt)
The light of Allah is the best,
For centuries, even the stars are aware of Allah (swt) light,
The night is lit by starlight,
To keep the devils away.
Glory to Allah (swt)

---

[9] Translation of the previous poem

Shamim Razaq

Mere Ghar Mein Ek Udassi Chaye Hai

Mere Ghar Mein Ek Udassi Chaye Hai
Ekh khamoshi ek ada bassi,
Mere ghar mein mere watan ki mahek se waqaf nahin,
Lakh bar koshish ki isse kaise mein apne watan ki khanni sunno,
Kaise woh mahek phool mahel sajoa,
Mere watan ki mitti mujhe doondthi
Bolti hai,
Ke pagli –
Waha nahin yahaan aa kar yahaan
Ke phool se apna ghar sajao
Mere watan ki ekh anmol, chand sifarish
Ek alag shaan,
Mere nanni, nanna, daddi dadde ki asal pehcaan,
Jin ka khoon pasina
Jin ki chaoon, jin ki soch se mein pali bassi,
Jin ke hathon se mein ne sikha pyar ka paigham.
Ab toh mere khwab mein bhi aane lage,
Jamun ki hawa aur titliyoon ki pehchaan ban kar,
Chaand sitaare ki roshni mein mujhe
Janat dikhane lage,
Beti –
Dekko, yahaan humaare watan mein
Hain humara khoon pasina bassa,
Tum kyun ho akeli aur khud se bewafa,
Tumhaari zubaan ke geet aur
Tumhari hee ankhoon ke saje khwab hain

The Lotus Flower

In seh millo,
Sab Allah ki niyamat aur tehri
Khushi ke liye hain.
Khud ko bula diya tha dunya ki nafratton
Aur jang ki shatranj se,
Is liye wapas lauti hoon,
Apne dil ko dunya se bacha ke,
Apne watan ki pehchaan ban kar
Apne watan ki khushi, sar ankoon par
Sakoon ka saya ban kar,
Lauti hoon apne angaan mein
Phool laganne aur bachon ke sapne
Ko awaz ki roshni dikhaane,
Jo bache din mein jal rahe hain
Unko raath ke sapne kaise meete lage geh,
Phir bhi chaand sitaare ki roshni mein,
Khuda ka rahem ke geet gaathe hain,
Eh mere watan math jalo paise ke khatir,
Yeh to kal ke Quais[10] hain.

---

[10] Imrus ul Quais was the first poet who created images with words in his poetry. Muhammad (pbuh) loved his poetry.

Shamim Razaq

There is a Strange Sadness in My Home[11]

There is a strange sadness in my home,
A silent spirit lives there,
My house is not aware of my country's aroma,
I tried a million times
In how I should tell my house the story of my country,
How do I adorn the house with perfumes and flowers.
The soil of my country is looking for me calling me
Hey,
Come and adorn your house
With flowers from here not from there.
My country has a priceless, moonlike unique pride,
Within its shadow within its thoughts I was nurtured,
In its hands I learnt the message of love.
Now they come in my dreams,
With an identity of a violet wind and butterflies,
In the light of stars and the moon I am shown signs of heaven.
Daughter-
Look here our blood and sweat is here,
Why do you feel alone and betraying yourself,
Its your tongues song and your dreams are adorned here,
Meet them,
These are the blessings of Allah (swt) and for your happiness.
I had forgotten myself in this worlds hatred and the war game,
That's why I have come back,

---

[11] Translation of the previous urdu poem.

Saving my heart from the world,
To be an identity for my country,
To be a calm spirit for the happiness of my country,
I have come back to my house,
To plant seeds and to teach children the light of dreams,
The children that burn daily in the heat of the sun
How will they find dreams sweet?
But still in the light of the moon and stars,
They sing the song of gratefulness to their Allah (swt).
Listen my country, stop burning for money,
These children are tomorrows visionaries.

Shamim Razaq

Jeena bhi Jihaad hai

Manzil doondthe doondthe,
khud ko talaash karna bhool gaye,
Pyar ki chahat mein, dunya ko pyar sikhana bhul gayee,
Ab toh ekh khwaish hain,
Dunya ke bachoon ke liye jeeyun,
Dil ki dunya mein, mein ne saja liya
Phooloon ka diya,
Joh har khushi gham mein saath yaad aathe hain,
In khi khas khushboo ki khas khoobsoorati hain,
Jo Allah (swt) ki ibaadat mein hain,

Tasbeeh ka har ekh moti ki thara
Mere watan ka eik eik bacha anmol heera hai,
Jo dunya ke rang aur khuda ki zameen
Par phool chamak rahe hain,
Dunya ke liye jeena pare toh lakh bar mehrbaan,
Khud ke liye jeena pare toh Allah ki rahoon ko doondthi peerthi hoon,
Jaise saans se zindagi aur khuda se salah hai,
Marne ke baad jaanat khuda ke bandoo
Ke liye ghar hain
Allah (swt) ka paigham pohchanna hain –
Jeena bhi is dunya mein jihad hai.

Isi liye zinda hoon.
Isi liye zinda hoon.

Living is to Thrive and Struggle in Allah (swt) Way[12]

Trying to find my destination,
I had forgotten to find myself,
In the need of love I forgot how to teach the world love,
Now I only have one wish,
To live for the children of the world,
In the world of hearts I have lighted a candle made of flowers,
That remembers you in happiness and sadness,
There is a unique aroma and a unique beauty
Which is in praise of Allah (swt)
Like every pearls of my tasbeeh,
Every child in my country is a priceless pearl,
That are shining in the colours of the world flowers.

If I have to live for myself I go searching for Allah (swt) way,
The way breath is to life, salah is to Allah (swt)
After death heaven is the house for the people of Allah (swt)
I have to pass a message from Allah (swt)
Living is to struggle and thrive in Allah (swt) way

That is why I am alive.
That is why I am alive.

---

[12] Translation of the previous urdu poem.

Shamim Razaq

Watan ki Pehchaan Ban kar

Dunya seh shikwa na karoon
Isi liye Allah (swt) ne mere dil ko dunya
Ke liye narm bana diya,
Aur ibadat mein shaamil kar ke
Auzaar karar diya.
Sabz pathon ka paani,
Aur phool ka maheka hua pasina,
Pakistan ka hara mausam hain,
Din ka suraj aur raat ke sitaare chamakte hain,
Goongunathe hain meri soch ko meri awaz ko,
Khuda ki khoobsoorati ka ehsas hai,
Sajde mein dil jookhta hain, pal pal
Subhan Allah, Alhamdulillah pukartha hain,
Har rang ke phal saje bazaar mein
Apni pehchaan aur khushboo se,
Dekh kar sar juktha hain
Apne watan ki mitti ki taqat par,
Jo har mausam ka phal aur har mausam ki sabzi
ki khushboo aur mithas zindagi ka hissa hain.

Drakht ki chaaon mein
Aur dil ki kahaani dadhkan bana kar behti hoon
Ekh khamosh musqurahat le kar,
Apne watan ki pehchaan ban kar.

Being an Identity for my Country[13]

So I don't complain to the world
Allah (swt) has made my heart weak for the world
And in prayer strong.
The water of the green leaves
And the flowers aroma like sweat
Is the green colour of Pakistan,
The daily sun and the stars shine,
Play tunes to my thinking and to my voice,
Aware of Allah (swt) beauty,
My head touches the ground time to time
Glory and praise to Allah (swt)
Every colour of every vegetable is displayed in the city,
With their own identity and aroma,
Looking at them I bow down,
At the strength of the soil in my country,
For producing every kind of fruit and vegetables.
Being part of life.

I'm sitting under the tree with my heartfelt story as heartbeats,
With a quiet smile
Being an identity for my country.

---

[13] Translation of the previous urdu poem.

Shamim Razaq

Ekh Khamosh Hissa

Zindagi ka ekh khamosh hissa,
Kissi ki yaad mein,
Kissi ki khwaish mein,
Kache daage ki thara,
Zindagi kab sath toot chor jaye,
Kisi koh kya khabar,
Khuda ke lafzoon ka sahara le kar,
Tasbeeh ka daaga leh kar,
Band rahi hoon, toot na jaye,
Khuda se farmaan hain,
Is ki dhor lambhi ho,
Khuda ke khatir,
Khuda aur nabi ki ibadat karni hain,
Dil ka sahara aur soch ki roshni le kar
Betti hoon, sochne lagi,
Har aurat ki apni kahaani,
Jo khamosh hain,
Khuda ka sahara le kar
Chup se rohna sikha,
Agar awaz ka haq milta,
Dunya ko apni kahaani soonathi,
Dil pe hath rakh kar,
Goongunathi apne ansoo.

Bol.

Aurat ko be izzat aur neecha dikha kar
Us par zulm karein,
Aur tawaif bana ke khote mein
Mast ankhoon ke hawaale karein,
Yeh kaun sa kanoon hain,
Kaisa insaaf,
Jo aurat khoon ke ansoo paani bana ke piyye.
Maryam pe kiye huein zulm,
Abhi bhi kanoo mein awaz ban kar,
Dil ko choohte hain,
Dukhoon ki parchaiyn mein,
Faryaad ban kar humein maa, beti, behen
Ke roop mein hijaab pehnaathe hain,
Pathe joh dhoop se dur aur andhere mein safed rang pehen le
Unka bhi khuda hain,
Jo sab Rangoon ka ek rang bana ke
Hijaab pehna kar dunya aur akhirat mein bhi
Maqam diya.
Subhan Allah; Alhamdulillah.

Shamim Razaq

A Quiet Part of Life[14]

There is a quiet part of life
In memory of someone,
A wish for someone,
Like the weak thread,
Nobody knows when life will end,
Who knows,
I took aid in Allah (swt) words,
I took the tasbeeh thread,
I'm tying it so it does not break,
I have a request to Allah,
That the thread remains long,
For the sake of Allah (swt),
I need to praise Allah (swt) and his messenger,
I took the company of my heart and the light of my ideas,
I'm sitting here thinking
Every woman has her own story,
Which is quiet,
With the help of Allah (swt)
I learnt to cry silently,
If I had the right to a voice
I would tell my story to the world,
Putting my hand on my heart
I would sing out tears,

---

[14] Translation of the previous urdu poem.

Speak.

Degrading women
And torturing them
And turning them into whores
In front of devils eyes
What justice is this?
Where women drink tears of blood
The torturing of Maryam
Still I hear that touches my heart,
In the shadow of sorrowness,
As a loud cry
They wrap every mother, daughter and sister in hijab,
The leaves that don't gain any colour in the sunlight
But gain the white colour in darkness,
Allah (swt) is aware of them,
As he made all the colours into one
And gave them that colour in the form of hijab
In this world and the next,
Glory and praise be to Allah (swt).

Shamim Razaq

Lafzoon ka Sahara Le Liya

Ek khanni hai pyar ki,
Jo bulai thi khuda ki,
Dohno basse ek alag des mein,
Lekin hawa ekh thi khushboo ki pehchaan bhi,
Pyar jo dunya ki khatir tha,
Suraj ke roop mein ekh diya jal raha tha,
Payal chanak rahi thi pyar ki awaz mein,
Titliyoon ki baarish, parindo ka saya tha
Falak ki chaoon pe,
Khuda ka paigham tha,
Sawaan muhabbat ka,
Dil pe chaya tha sitaron ki roshni,
Soch mein mahel saja tha,
Ankhon me thi abaadi.

Insaniyat ki niyat
Jo dekh na saka – dunya ki khaq mein jal jaye ga,
Usko zindagi ki kya khabar thi,
Jo aag mein jalna seekh le,
Unko khuda ki rehmat kha naseeb thi,
Dilu mein jalan aur tanhaai na ho,
Khuda ne apna maqam qarar diya,
Ibadat karne walo ka hath tham liya
Nananuweh naam khuda ke,

The Lotus Flower

Allah ka naam le kar Insaniyat ko ekh bana diya,
Aag jo paharoon se ugthi hain,
Shole jo aatish fishah se ugthe hain,
Unki bhi ek roshni hain,
Phool jo pathar se nickle,
Unki bhi ek khushboo hain,
Dunya ki khaq mein jo jal jaye,
Unko phoolon ki kya khabar thi,
Jo khud aag mein jal jaaye
Unko Khuda ki rehmat kahan naseeb thi,
Jab sochne lagi Khuda ka naam badnaam na ho,
Khamosh ho kar lafzoon ka sahara le liya.

Shamim Razaq

I Took the Support of Words[15]

There is a story about love,
Which was the call of Allah (swt),
They both lived in different countries,
But the wind was the same, so was the fragrance,
Their love was for the world,
In the form of the sun, a hope was lit,
The anklet was twinkling with the sound of love,
There was a rainstorm of butterflies and shadows of birds,
In the sky,
There was Allah (swt) message,
It was the season of love,
The stars were shining in the heart,
A palace was built in thoughts,
And there was life.

The one who could not understand the human intentions,
Will be buried in the ashes of the world,
What did he know about life,
Who learnt to burn in the heat,
They were not blessed by Allah (swt) blessings.

---

[15] Translation of the previous urdu poem.

The Lotus Flower

So that people don't burn and live in loneliness,
Allah (swt) declared his place,
He held the hand of worshippers,
Ninety nine names of Allah,
By saying Allah he united humanity,
The fire that comes out of mountains,
And the fireworks from rocks,
They have light too,
The flowers that grow from rocks,
They have a fragrance too.

The ones who burn in the world,
They were not aware of the fragrance of the flower,
The ones who burn themselves in the world,
They are not aware of Allah (swt) blessings,
So that Allah (swt) name does not get a bad name,
I took the support of words.

Shamim Razaq

Searching for Sweetness

A humming bird; A jewel with wings,
Sits on the sweet scent of a butterfly bush,
Ruby throated, to the branch, it clings,
With vibrant colours and tiny trumpet like flowers.

Summers breeze kisses it as it passes,
As wings hum as it hoisters higher,
The luminous pink attract its tiny eyes,
The sharp, adapted bill ordered, to feed on the life giving drink.

A butterfly, a symbol of renewal and beauty,
Joins him at the Keys of Heaven,
With bulbous, bouncy blooms, big and bright,
As they share the holy drink in the garden.

A Wild Romance is at the far end,
With dancing bees and marching ants,
Butterflies and the jewels with wings,
Dancing the long, languid days.

The sun shines on, the rhythm continues,
The equilibrium erupts many moments,
All rolled into one extraordinary exposure,
As the creator views his show.

Battle of Mind and Soul

Both sides of sentiments are of importance,
They are there for the good and kind,
Like nature with its diseases,
Nothing would move: Nothing would bind.

Religion is a belief; a faith within,
That grows and keeps you away from sin.
The sunflower would not grow,
If the sun didn't rise with its shiny glow,

Indulgent intellects and poisonous passions,
Are inside like force and gravity,
Self belief will grow in confidence,
Giving in will break the sovereignty.

Understanding the sentiments,
Will perforate the intellect,
It's all within the mortal,
To rise and self correct.

Read Aloud

Praying salah and reciting Qu'ran,
Keeps devil inflicted and acquired sin away,
As tears run and give pure relief in the wind,
These tears become rivers and streams. They warp into yarn.

Reading aloud helps you understand better,
Internal connections flourish the external connections,
As each word has depth—so does each letter,
This liberates much peace, love and affections.

The Story of The Ant

I am a social, sterile wingless creature,
Some use me in pest control agents,
So I am also an earth bleacher,
And wasps are my historical descendants.

My antennae's are prostrated and my weight is light,
I work in groups, but my duty is great,
For my use and means are right,
I have been awarded eight times my weight.

I can solve complex problems,
And I modify habitats.
I have expanded like the flowering plant,
And I cover a mass of earths land.

Shamim Razaq

An Invitation

Journey: The freedom of Mind
Dedicated to my mum, grandmother and mother in law and all the women of the world.

THE journey I took back to education,
Was believing: where there is vision, lives a dream,
A dream to grow, a dream to thrive,
A freedom of faith. A freedom of mind.

Women in Kashmir: Women in Asia,
Women in Nepal; Women in India,
Women from diverse walks of life,
And women from mentally tortured lives.

I invite—make this fulfilling journey,
Of freedom of feelings and expression,
Come back to education to gain knowledge,
Because educated women, educate the family.

The Lotus Flower

Make this a reality to spread an educated life,
This system of second class has to end,
STOP! Being the liquid,
Taking the shape of the bottle,
Stop the prophecy that sets a negative trend.

The journey of a woman is based on her intuitive nature,
That commands, comprehends, and communicates,
The journey from a dedicated daughter doing the deed,
To a mother, her children she capacitates.

A woman is the creativity of this world,
Her journey is a lifetime, that has to make its way,
The journey that does not end at death,
But continues for all she has left educated
and shown the way.

Shamim Razaq

A Woman in The Third World

In a carpet of corn and crops,
In a third world alien land
A lady works hard wiping her teardrops,
And serving people in the modern land.

Her silver chalice is her only prize,
As she drinks the liquid aluminium,
As the earth grows in front of her eyes,
She is a fine example of altruism.

Her days are the same and duty is repeated,
In the blades of grass and of woven fields,
Her task will never be completed,
She carries on and on in the nurturing land – heated.

The dream to visit the modern land remains a dream,
A dream she sees but real for her grain,
She puts all her hopes in with shaft of heat,
Making seedlings grow with rays of rain.

Women Weaving *Garb(age)*

The war used and abused the women,
They weren't spared of their dignity,
Not even of their self respect and identity,
Fragile, torn and exposed to obscenity,
It begins at home where she has the right to security,
It became mode and a self fulfilling prophecy,
As the devil in the man robs her spirituality,
The prison punishes moral crimes,
In these ladies years of Prime,
Locked up they feel free,
What world is this
Where women are turned into debris?
They walk in a blue, damask, burqa bubble,
So they don't end up in serious trouble,
The International society has dumped them, they fear
But little they know they adorn in hearts that heed them dear.

Living a low life is their expectancy,
Shockingly, dying at forty four averagely,
Majority are forced into marriages,
Then they are faced with many challenges,
Where living means disadvantages,
Diamond like, silk like lotus ladies live with no rights,
Where hope is petite shedding little light,

Shamim Razaq

On the floor ants work together,
In the hot summer weather,
Afghanistan has the highest rate of widowhood,
And tiny, little girls poisoned in their childhood,
Childhood is a time of dreaming,
Childhood is a time of weaving,
It's a time when magic seedlings,
Begin to grow and find their place,
When all the knots are tied,
The eyes are opened wide,
Childhood goes out to play,
Childhood deserves to go out and play,
The wonders that occur are endless,
Each moment should be priceless,
But in this patch of the world
Women cannot escape the violence,
They are forced to marry her rapist,
She then becomes a devoted feminist,
Takes the opportunity to stand up for justice,
A duty a drive to demolish prejudice,
Weaving a strong base and decreasing wrinkles,
30 years has been reduced to widows and orphans,
Now they have been given lighter sanctions,
In hope for a positive, fairer role,

The Lotus Flower

Be it in business or be it politics,
Women want to achieve academics,
Be it tailoring or be it independence,
Seams have to be stronger, and clothes have to fit
A society has to be built,
This is every womans birth right,
To weave a future that's portrayed bright.

Within their craft they will fix, they will mend,
They will shuttle a positive trend,
Within their craft they will fix, they will mend,
They will shuttle a positive trend.

They want to take garbage out of garb age,
So they devote and make a stand,
Hoping people will finally understand,
Under the veiled clothe,
Is a mother, sister, wife or daughter with peace and warmth,
They have a hu(e)man soul like you and I,
Don't let this patch of the world die.

Shamim Razaq

Excuse a Poetess in Salwar Kameez and Dupatta as she Talks about Voices

Excuse me if I have multiple cultural voices,
You see, the sea came from one voice,
The voice of our ancestors,
From Adam and Eve to my kids,
Any one voice can come out at anytime,
Any place, anywhere,
My emotions change throughout the day
My voice changes with my emotions,
I come in layers,
But from the same soul,
I walk with my words,
Like you walk in yours,
A poets world fits all sizes,
No matter size, colour or shape,
It catwalks many voices, because
We are many,
But we all are a unity,
In the global community,
We try on voices,
And keep the ones that fit,
For some one, but for others many.

The Peak of Light

When she was born,
A star was born,
Covered in a pure white cloth,
With shining blinking eyes,
She had nothing to offer but a smile so wise,
A joy of her security, innocence and love,
Wrapped like a white feathered dove.

As she became older,
A complex case of unanswered questions,
and emotions overtook,
The security slipped away,
Like mercury slipping away with time
And the joy was no longer there.
A world of mishaps began to take shape,
And there was no escape
From the electrified paths,
To technology sending vibes across many mediums,
Across lines that became larger than life,
The television dictates in its corner,
Where it is worshipped day and night,
Knowingly or not, nobody knows,
She tried to keep up with the world,
With its technological game,
Her inferiority grew parallel with the technology.

Shamim Razaq

Venus has genes similar to our earth,
Sisters in space, and sisters by fate,
You are closer to the sun, yet you are colder,
I am closer to nature, yet I am inferior,
Why is there this disparity?
The life giving queen bee squeaks,
And the irony of death head also squeaks,
Why is there this similarity?
When we are full of complexities?
Is my language mind more complicated than me?
Is the world more simple than we make it to be?
Most people live in the world that has been scribed,
But heaven is for only worshippers prescribed,
Who believe in the unseen.

She carries on living in contradictories,
Establishing worship away from the temporary world,
Some mock and say she is mad,
As she repels from earthly beings,
Many backgrounds she has stood up front,
But who can decide her true colour,
Because life is full of shades, tones and histories.

The Lotus Flower

What nature is this?
When she is in a body temporarily suitable for earth,
Like a caterpillar cocooned for renewal and rebirth?
Is it because the sun has not reach its peak
Is it because humanity has not reached
The highest point of intellect
In shedding light to the world?

Descendants of Adam and Eve

They were innocent—and then heard the whisper,
Of the unseen devil, that travelled and breathed through the air,
breathing in every man and woman and has cherished deeper,
Through generations with feelings of Eves unsecurity and despair.

Some poets have praised her with physical beauty,
While others have called her a creature,
Some have labelled her as a witch or a Barbie doll,
While others have abused, mocked her and mother nature.

Some have buried her alive, very young,
While others turned her into a commodity,
Some have burnt her alive or had her hung,
But a few have recognised her identity.

Adam stands a tremendous trial,
In the evolution of the human brain,
He grows in sensitivity or in utter brutality,
As the world continues to fight the obedience campaign.

Some prostrate and glorify God,
While others live in only darkness,
But claim to be enlightened with worldly fame,
And some remain level to the earth and know why they came.

Sacred Flower—Love is not Enough

I sat down and shed sundrops from my bloodshot eyes,
As they turned to ashes, I cried deaf, dumb and blind,
My blood wept away from my veins,
As people abuse and drill holes into the human frame,
I felt weak and moribund, I sat and undone my minds sum,
The Black swan rises within me with white plummage,
And the mocking bird within me sings human killing is a sinful abusage.

My lovemind had changed and my energy increased in multiples,
I fast and abstain from death and increase life,
As one night is equal to a thousand months,
I plead to people stop these marionette of man made deaths,
Oppressions of women will become oppressive, internalised dark cages,

Be it Syria, Afghanistan or be it Africa,
Be it the developed page or be it the empty lines of space,
Be it Palestine, Burma, Iraq or Jamiaca,
People have been used, abused and displaced.

Einsteins artificial nature is killing the human nature,
With the fireball, sundrop like bombs bringing judgement day closer,
As bombers roam with rifles witness the final day,
Why are they blind to it when they demonstrate the final role play?

When I lost all my hope and my curious mind became furious,
My soul asked, 'What's in the cube, what's in the Ka'ba?'
I went online and discovered the seven sacred hanged poems,
Hanged inside the Ka'ba, poems of love before prophet Muhammad (pbuh),
Came on this lovestruck sick earth,
My blood began to run violet and green, and I felt serene,
Imru-ul-Quais creator of images,
Muhammad (pbuh) loved his visionaries,
I see through the same lens, learnt pure love is a disease, (what contradiction)
Weak as the silk of the spiders web, but still strong enough,
To save prophet Muhammad
As Allah promised humanity in the most simplest fashion,
True love is the highest act of worship on the sacred world grid,
That needs to be bleached and cleansed,
The sacred heptagonal, hive like flower remains a symbol of life,
Dear land pure love is not enough for this world.

The Lotus Flower

The ka'ba represents the time of Abraham,
Inside it is a spirit of religious purity,
Like us women who choose to wear the hijab
And circulate in our daily mind and gain spiritual power,
I want to fly seven times round, fly like a dove,
But there are no tears left in me,
Dry as salt and weak as glass,
My blood has turned into rust,
My immense love is small in this big world.
I rise and I read,
Childrens fate torn early, Daughters graves dug early,
I have been buried early, I'm a dead soul searching,
With a heart that thumps tears of love and blood.

Shamim Razaq

The Lone Dandelion

My soul rising and reclaiming for a daily death,
As I see mothers breathe daily blight and mournful breaths,
And families exposed to social barbaric diseases,
Fledging flocks of families fragile to gunshots,
And innocent eyes betrayed by rays of bloodshots,
Degraded daughters are transported to human trafficking,
Then raped, burnt and butchered by household judges,
Prophesising and moulding into an external trait, trammel and trademark,
And Asian world maps are blotted with gamed, scored bloodspots.

Bombs and shells clash and smoke people into hostile air,
Fathers' visions of rising stars have combusted to falling stars and firestorms,
As the moon and strange stars watch the sun burning young flowers,
With death and blood storms on timed faces instead of freedom and eternal hours,
Wrapped and displayed on world wide web as final products,
For people to glance the final frame, but not to hear the cries, or feel the pains,
Slaughtered children lie dead amongst the whispering timeless soil with blood stains.

Where once they sculpted ritual dreams in the lonely deserts sands,
With innocent eyes, growing hands and daily visions,
If only they knew sculptures in dry sand soon blow away without any strand,
Now all that remains is scrunched up dead bodies, blood timed and inert,
Mothers madly laugh through jaundiced faces
They say justice has been done and there *jaan* is in heaven,
But their motherly green nature and hurting violet hearts,
Have been ruptured and torn in many parts,
Mothers hands tied in sensory cells and devils infected territory.

The veins coil, twist and turn in weak frames and threaten human lifespan,
As dispersed children beg food in naked, snaked paths destroyed and disturbed homeland,
Knowing not if their day will shower shells crack sea shells or brainstorm bombs,
As they calm together in a corner of the canopy night with poor palms.
In another corner of the world there is a lone silver seeded,
Dandelion under a grey cloud,
Between the thin green leaves of a writers lined blank book,
Wishing the seeds of the dandelion to fly over,
To that part of the world and grow leaflets of hope.

Shamim Razaq

I Am Walking

I am walking Arithmetic breeze,
With my friends in cool warm breeze,
Holding our written dreams and visions close to chest,
Like the roots in the soil spreading, i'm growing in knowledge
Breathing out love and laughter, away from the prince of darkness,
In our eyes and in our hearts we flower flourished liberation,
Writing out our own future, with the blood of our pen,
We will never cry
But live and expand our beauty and colour.

The bullet shot mail paralyzying my emotions inside black,
My body went into deep sleep coma,
As my soul white light ignites and begins repair,
Senseless and inert my senses,
Takes timeout to reconnect to nature,
The thundering healing light repairs genetic tissue,
The machines magic beat my black heart out softly as the roar of thunder,
Praying and glorifying Allah in the absence of my senses.
The creepy wires run electric blood through my veins,
Turning me to death in this artificial game,
My soul fights for soul and light,

Mummy like militants stand with vampire armours
Hungry for pure blood that carries peace and freedom,
Walking on the deathly roads named jihads of Taliban,
Thirsty for love and peace of the enlightened,
To trap it all in blackness.
The Qu'ran teaches humanity,
The highest point of worship to fight forward,
But people rather follow the actions,
Rather see through the light of the book,
It is the light that carries you forward.

Shamim Razaq

Walk of Life

Many roads and streets come in the way,
In the never ending world of walk of life,
Sometimes they end; sometimes they open another way,
Sometimes they twist and turn into a strife.

But there is light at the end of a tunnel,
And every step taken had a meaning,
So don't take things too personal,
Because without losing there is no achieving.

One day will come – you'll walk down memory lane,
When you'll look back and see all the connections,
Like connected neurons, the walks will look like a brain,
Your life had been mapped out and memories have turn into reflections.

Nine Eleven

Nine eleven changed the world for the worst,
It shaped a society of terror and violence,
It degraded humanity and labelled people cursed,
And turning humanity vulnerable to arrogance.

A decade later the stigma remains,
But slowly through media things begin to change,
What was claimed is now being reviewed,
And I hope that humanity sees a change.

The numbers: nine eleven mean different to me,
I did my research and found the truth,
The numbers mean more than a title as you will see,
In the following lines that will speak the truth.

The number nine symbolises extent and revolving around,
When cubed it shows spiritual achievement,
So why are numbers misunderstood in Gods Ground,
Why did the world live all this time in bereavement?

I understand that thousands died and families were torn,
But that was a reaction from people who suffered more,
By thinking one way new ideas will never be born,
So see it as a learning curve and an end to war.

The number eleven symbolises intuition,
Patience, honesty and sensitiveness,
Eleven is the peacemaker in action,
And strengthened by insights, peace, love and gentleness.

The day could have been titled differently,
But why was it titled nine eleven
Was it a coincident or a done deliberately?

The world is not meant to be a fictional Utopia,
Because conflict began at the beginning of humanity,
People should come to common terms in the global sphere,
Perfection is not a solution because people need to grow creatively.

Prince of Darkness

19th October 2012

Betwixt[16] the covers and between the heart and mind,
He whispers in her ear about nafs[17] and purifying heart and mind,
She lay down serene, restored by spiritual verses of natures light
After salah, but the prince of darkness damned whispers deaths knell,
And his magnitude, madcap nature burning touch turns blood into haemorrhage hell,
In the blackness of magic macabre the combusted acid rain burns green,
The maiden head on the pink pillow, looks at shutters of blind black bean,
Rolling shiny tasbeeh beads between fingers blessed.

He looked at her white, white face with his catatonic hang over obsessed,
Dissolving back into the dark with eyes filled melancholy,
His devil, device eyes move away from her doe eyed drops body,
As she restores her natural beauty and spirituality,
She turns away glorifying like acid thunder in Allahs praised rainstorm,
She dwells into deep visions of isolated heavenly brainstorms,
As her soul is taken away to the heights of skies,
She silences her breaths and closes her purified eyes.

---

[16] Between

[17] Intention

The morning dew looks back at eyes chrome green,
The maiden with hands of beauty spots and breath of caffeine,
Smiles at natures fine nose friendly musk and mother natures scene,
As piano keys play gentle crisp music, she covers her spine with soft ebony hair,
Light feet crumble crisp spicy leaves as her hijab covers her modesty and features fair,
She slowly walks in distilled air holding tight onto heaven scent dream soul,
With lowered trees from the violet nightfall she blends in with Allahs call.
Walking salah days in visions of emerald and violet waterfall.

In the evening coming of autumn golden nightfall,
She listens to rhythms and dwells in sweet sixteen snowfall,
Where she had known spring buds will bloom in midsummer light,
She waited for him to come before her eyes,
But came the prince of darkness besotted in disguise,
Years went by, she had grown true, strong and full of faith,
She begged him to treat her like a mortal and not a mental wraith.

The Lotus Flower

She understood the evil eye and curse was casted on her,
As family foundations were fragmented in historical blurs,
She cried 'Why me? Why punish me? When i am true to my soul,'
With energetic negative vibes cursed, emotions were out of control,
They mocked and robbed her wisdom and her strength,
She broke into isolated violent wavelengths,
I will become half paralysed and my life will be numb,
She prays to Allah, to complete her life divine love to come.

Shamim Razaq

Every Strip has a Silver Lining – Gaza

Less is more when more has been taken away,
Rocket radiated, letter bombed, shell shocked as i write to express more
The drugged up curse caused a stir in my minds eye,
As i spun round in a bout, soul searching the essence of life,
Where people see the world through a stigmatised glass as graphic art,
My deconstructed mind and my deconstructed heart,
Began to find reason beyond the parameters of my universe,
Found my soul crying in cages of human so-called norms articulating verse.

As days in Gaza are highlighted by fragmentation bombs,
Mothers of white skin growing green as murderers atomize red and black,
Children cry collecting dry twigs burning, burying dead dreams in small palms,
Or drawing visions and images of heavenly colourful homes on paper plaques,
As teenagers hearts clutch the wired bordered fence wanting to live the highlife,
Gazing into the distance to dance the language of Gaza life,
To go beyond the parameters of physical borders,

Instead being rooted in sandy seas of flooded dead bloody soils –

The Lotus Flower

Children are the hopeful force behind deathly days, faces fair full of grace,
But when death creeps coming close children are full of woe,
Crying woe to the oppressors, feeling they still have far to go,
Working laborious hours day in day out so love can be grown,
And homes turn into fruitful heavens with art tapestry sewn.

As battling winter brings haemorrhage war to temporary freeze,
Spring brings a ray of happiness and days to pursuit buoyant breeze,
Letter bombs are replaced by world record kite days,
Showing all colours hue by the summer water line,
Dreams that were buried early, come out to play near the silver line,
Where children fly their dreams or build sandcastles –
Dreams combined,
Carrying psychedelic light so dreams can survive and thrive,
In this land that is currently bruised, burnt and buried alive.

Shamim Razaq

Parts of Pakistan

(Dedicated to the innocent victims of October 2011 attacks)

What strange weather this season has bought,
What strange feelings arise between you and i,
This October heat wave sends a warmth in my heart,
What about you? You are forever frozen and mute
As if you are fighting a battle within,
Like nature battling away the heatwave,
That stole the warmness of Autumn,
Or is it like the annual virus wanting to make its way.

'I am fine, just understanding my art within,
Wondering where does it stand and what does it mean.'
'Can I help? I'm already set free from my words.'
'I will read, listen to the tales of the unknown,
The deathly victims are innocent in the battle of the bloods
The youth die in their days of joy and love,
My country suffers a sea of blood and floods,
What has happened to my country in which I lived and loved,
Politicians are talking like programmed robots,
Not wanting to re-establish humanity with its joys.'
'Pakistan has been flooded and bloodied,
It is a view of a collapsed country that is being studied,
And that has had a natural disaster

The Lotus Flower

As water has become peoples grave,
Like a nervous breakdown of the human soul and brain,
With your head in your hands buried down in your own salty water,
Where there is no way out of the heated oppression,
Where even your shadows have been burnt in the compression,
To the ground in the heat of the sun and heart domination,
Where once the shadows prostrated in prayer to Allah,
Now every catchment area is draining blood
The men, women and children open their book like hands
And pray in reconciliation to their Allah.
The streets look like an interminable mine sweep,
With human debris and *Kachra*[18] making people weep
Where push the button has become a game
Slicing bodies and lighting flames,
In another corner a police man in pins and needles madly
Beats the spirit out of a manual worker
As broken bodies witness soul slaughter.
Magma like boiling blood
Creeps out from their bodies onto the surface,
The undone jigsaw,
Of body compartments are audible human murmurs
As they slither on the salted, soiled and sandy ground.

---

[18] Urdu word for debris

Shamim Razaq

The drone like dragonflies swarm and surge through the air,
Curious of the people who have nothing to declare,
The visionary dragonflies fly like a helicopter hovering,
They look in the depth of the human soul searching and discovering,
They devote their matured wisdom in living for the now,
Opening the divine human mind and conscious they bestow
Their lives have been mainly in the depths of water with the lotus,
Their eyes are deep and can see things holistically,
So next time you see one, don't shoo it away.

Prophet Nuh's ark gushed out the sins from the sinners,
And everything was started a new,
So see this as a sign from above,
The creator is giving you a chance to love,
Take it with your book like hands and see what happens,
I'm sure things will resolve for the better,
Trust more in Allah than man, Because man can let you down.
The daffodil will spring out, the summer sun will simmer,
The sunburnt leaves will die and the cold will snip and bite.
As seasons change to relate to the inner human battle.
My country is springing blood and burning summer,
And dying like leaves as snowball,
Like bombs snip and bite the already beaten, bitten skin.

I cannot bear to witness this, what will I tell my lord?
That i sat there watching the box but i did nothing
Because I fear fate of martyrdom?

They entered the world not knowing their destiny
But destiny knew their destination,
They were over loaded with external brutality and sensitivity
They burst and diffused in the atmosphere
Leaving movement for others to follow.

No mother nature gives birth to a martyr
The international human society creates them
To make life move, everything is in
The movement of one's soul this is one of the characteristics of life.
MRS GREN how I remember you today,
The reproduction of martyrs is growing,
Along with martyr sensitivity and bittersweet
Sugar releasing chemicals from the body,
And expelling people poisoned people from the face of the planet,
As new souls nourish the goodness for growth and repair.
But how long will this last? I ask a question fair,
Who has the answer?
Humanity or does the answer lie with the voice of human nature?

Shamim Razaq

What is beyond the Sky?

What is beyond the sky is a great mystery,
We are told: there are lots of planets and galaxies,
Planets: some rocky, some fiery and some icy
A different time, a different place with eternities.

A star is conceived by a nebulae, so near yet so far,
Which ignites and explodes a bright gas, spreading far,
It looks a spectacular round centre with magic fairy dust,
Sadly to say, this is when I tell you the other side.

The bigger the star, the sooner it will subside
The bigger the mass, the sooner it will lose its pride,
Turn dust to dust, ashes to ashes, our shiny guide.

It is a wonder that all the planets orbit around the Sun,
The suns gravity holds planets in place and spectrum
And all planets, stars and moons keep momentum.

The Autumn sunflower turns to the sun,
That the moon purifies the sea at night,
That there is life at the core of the sea,
That there is something opposite and greater than the earth.

The Lotus Flower

Where cosmic winds are at play,
Where new stars Inflate, burst and originate,
Our rocky planets: Mars, Earth, Mercury, and Venus,
Our gas giants: Jupiter, Saturn, Neptune and Uranus.

All unique with magical madness and mystics,
All different with hopeful and living characteristics,
Nobody knows the ultimate fate of the universe
Is it doomed, destined or will it end in tragic disperse.

Shamim Razaq

The Sun

I am the symbol of life,
And I rise with intensity,
I make the dark become the light,
And my shaft of light showers felicity.

I am the large globe of hydrogen and helium gas
That nurtures and fuels life on earth;
Without me the world would collapse,
And there would be no mortal or mirth.

I am the delightful rich provider,
That twinkles in transient gold.
I am the hand that makes your food and grain
And send positive vibes with my universal power.

My fireworks are at play,
The roar of my flames are extreme:
It is a feeling of infinitude,
As I, the large ball of fire gleams and beams.

I am the one that follows your shadow,
And turns you away from my gaze,
I touch the earth with my hot hands,
And give you the best of my days.

The Sky at Night

(6th March 2012)

In a dream I saw,
Five other planets, I watched in awe
I sat in a field so light green,
With hills scurrying clouds so serene,
As the beacon casted down
Speckles of rich characteristics
From above became part of me.

I was attracted to the light,
As if my time has come to shine,
The night was enlightening indigo,
And strong smells of lavender
Sent waves of a spiritual force and of time,
Above the ground and to another level I beheld
My sight had not seen so much magnet force,
My dreams are closer to me.

Reality is so simple.

What wonderful fruits dreams are made of,
If only reality reflected so much light,
Showering many spectrums of wavelengths.

Sea

We cannot take the drops out of the sea,
Only add to them more,
Sit by the sea and let them rage and roar,
Let them speak about your hidden emotions,
Let your emotions join in and then let them go,
Carry on walking you will see diamond dazzles,
On the top of the furrowed dancing sea.

A delight will reach your eyes and bring on a smile,
Make this moment last as long as could be.
You will breathe better and deeper, you will sea,
Because you let go of what was caged inside
And joined the rhythm of the eternal sea.

You will look back, think,
Reflect and understand,
That was not too hard, all I did was breathe,
And felt a dark emptiness fill with inner peace.

Every Cloud has a Silver Lining

The Grey Clouds hang high in the sky,
Amongst the white and the black,
An anxiety attack of hue and cry
Will fall filling the human tear sac.

Or they will spread like pearls,
Like morning flourished dewdrops,
Tiptoeing on the ground in swirls and twirls,
Entering the soil that also shares the sundrops.

Helping plants to grow,
No matter the colour or the race,
They will work together in the soil below,
Resulting in beauty and eternal grace.

Shamim Razaq

Pacific Ocean

My emotions rise like the Pacific ocean,
Resulting in an underwater volcanic eruption,
In boiling magma fire like dust,
My feelings have to come to the surface.

Our feelings are important,
Leaving a deep impact on the world,
It only takes a few wit words,
To change the human world.

These words become fluid—floating
And travelling through the air,
Reaching high where they are most needed,
And they shower thoughts in your head.

Sometimes these come out as a word or
Ballad, poem, sonnet, ode
Or a lyrical melody
Refreshing and purifying
The emotional world and its longevity.

Survival

Earth needs loving care,
Hands to help it stay healthy,
Food keeps us healthy.

Artificials and
Chemicals can destroy the
Earth, like flavourings can.

Ammunition of
Mass destruction can destroy
The earth and people.

Technology can
Destroy the human nature
Why develop it?

Earth needs balance to,
Promote healthy life and growth,
Don't misuse technology.

Shamim Razaq

Evening colours

The evening suns colours casts heat waves in the sea,
All the way to the fine line where the sky and sea meet,
With rusty red, bulbous blue and vivacious violet
The emotions set alight as we walk the shoreline in clear view,
Which sways and rocks from time to time,
The silence is still, the waves quiet and tranquil,
The moment is warm, the wind is teasing
The moon is enduring while time is soothing.

Small Blue Flowers

The winds wails as it changes form to meet Autumn,
I sit here near the vibrating window as a welcomer,
Writing and then waiting for more words to come,
T o give me peace from the pall and death of summer,
As it awakens the sleeping autumn.

The storms that follow will bring the winter material furs,
The baby's wail warps in the wind,
But listen baby, there is hope like the earth in the dark dense universe,
Things will settle and new things will begin.

Forget me not as the writer inside me awakes in this time,
And like a beating heartbeat, the visions come in measured moments,
The twist brushes and smudges away summers fine lines,
Like an artist powdering off dust from his painting.

Shamim Razaq

The Sandcastle

The freedom of timeless fragrance never left the soil,
Because brown is the dominant eye colour,
It is the colour of all souls,
Every corner of the earth echoes and speaks it,
Shifting it, reclaiming it, sensing it, renewing it,
Shifting it, reclaiming it, sensing it, renewing it,
Eating from it and growing from it,
In these are reminders from Allah (swt),
The unity and the oneness of his creation,
In this simple timer which we call—dust.

Learn to turn soil into a timeless sense,
Instead of burnt ashes that will haunt,
For generations to come,
Build a sandcastle in the morning,
Dream with dignity, dwell in it,
And let nature wash it away,
With one fine stroke in the evening,
Because tomorrow never comes,
And your dreams will never fade away.

Dents in My Book

So fair, perceptive these summer colours
leaving dents in my book of leaves,
As the autumn bruises come to the tops of trees,
Beginning at the edge of maturity,
Finding their way to the core,
Tones of high pitch winds moan through the cooling air,
As they make their way to the land of trees and seas,
Seasoned leaves breathe in seasoned air,
The fireball in the high sky sends light,
And meditating insight sends heat to my eyes,
Opening a prime of sights and thoughts,
My heart is hurting letting go summer,
With its warm love colours hue,
As something kills my heart without a sound,
That was living, growing showing me a glow,
The fruits that fall fill my eyes with drops from heaven,
As I restore my minds eye,
Bringing hope back with the end of summer,
Accepting antique autumn and its affections,
Enriching colours adding heartbeat rhythm,
Warm, mature, muster of words,
Opening wings to a host of dreamers.

Shamim Razaq

Entwined

The white webbed twigs,
Glistening electric struck Royal stars,
Twinkling bulbous sky watches the festive season below,
The fun, the laughter, the warmth and the wishes made:
As the snow filled eyes, widen with diffracted light,
Entwined by the brilliance of polar daylight,
Standing here, living for a different time in place,
Labelled as solecism, in fantasy stimulating soporific sleep,
Still in nightspace, the stars twinkle,
And I stand here entwined,
Soon, the rhythm begins to settle in my heart,
With heartfelt words falling as my art,
I sit and recollect my lifes thoughts,
In cages of my lungs—tongued and purified breath,

Garden of Eternal Eden

Crowned with stars and echoing white opal
Glistening through crystal clusters of icicles,
As vibrations of white light heal the seven chakras,
Angelic spirits revive aquamarine teal globeflower,
Tasbeeh like rosary beads heal wintergreen mother nature,
Century old-seasoned crimson pomegranate tree,
Snow dropped gardenia gathered jewel stones,
Vibrate seasoned dyed emotions.

The peacock feathers.

The strong dew roots holding mother natures drops of tears,
Eyebright welcomes light window like morning glory of the snow,
The bird of paradise observes the snow capped mountains,
Rainbow spectrum of coloured beauty shining marigold sun,
Welcomes angel held lords and ladies with lavender aroma and lemon balm,
Buttercups, cabbage rose, sweet pea, tea rose –
Lit by water lily like high Chinese lanterns,
In the Garden of Eternal Eden

Shamim Razaq

Dare to Dream—To the Growing Ones

Dreams don't need forces of nature to make way for me,
Energy is all that's needed from the brain to see acuity,
My mirror in the mind sees beyond human control,
Bringing the confluence of logical sentiments to kaleidoscope scroll,
Where all forces are in play with the divine human soul.

The seven wonderful laws of universe,
Are put into force when Allah (swt) sows a mass of multiverse,
Giving out dreams that need to be grown with ground stored gravity,
With cloudbursts and encouraging nature spoken airwaves,
To bring his altruism insight as a real image flourishing results in life,
To eliminate evil, expanding potential dreams to new heights,
Vibrating good feelings attracting others to a beautiful sight,
The polarity of north south poles attracts good gravity in people,
As day follows night the centre of earth circulates seven spiritual times.

The Lotus Flower

In a nutshell, the clove at the end of natures cycle is used as a spice,
To heal what was hurt and taste its aromatic cycle life,
The warm walnut tree lays fruit bear as winter twigs freeze in air,
To heal the growing mind that will produce fruits from the brain,
The crescent cashew nuts bring dementia to a dead end,
But even the caged bird sings in times of death,
Opens its wings sings towards freedom,
Looking beyond the bars of its aviary,
With bronze plummage and gales of night in laughter,
Calling out to the gateway of heaven,
Where peahens wait for peaceful spirits,
With respect like Goldcrest filled gardens with Angels trumpets,
Or the morning dew frost, frozen in time of nature,
Walking through distilled air in winter landscape,
With warm caffeine breath wintersweet spice gems,
Spiralled inwards with natural colours fluoresced,
Nurtured along the grapevine of mother nature,
Producing talcum powder like winter fairy lights the garden,
Endangered by electric communication sending browbeat vibes,
With dreams so whitely rare and sleep so bipolar balanced,
Where everything is in motion—anything is possible.

Shamim Razaq

Paris

The city with endless lights and scope,
Like endless, emerging patterns in a kaleidoscope,
With its integrated buildings and colours hue.
Stand tall in the air of the river seine.

The miracle Eiffel tower that spreads vibes of love and beauty,
With many hearts having entered the river of love,
Many hearts it has reconciled in the name of its duty,
Many more it awaits for, to share its eternal love.

There is no limit to the magic and illusions,
From Fantasy land to rich heritage cultures,
From pyramids, paintings in La Louvre and Cathedrals,
With many shared prophecies and acculturations.

The polar crisp winter weather,
Preparing love and warmth for the nights,
At the famous tower with array of cosmic lights,
Without any religious intervention, lovers are blessed.

Anything is possible after this point,
Lovers leave in harmony hand in hand,
This will help their relationship, forever be strong,
Breathing the love in the air, as it blows its charms.

The Lotus Flower

The moment stood still as I looked from the Eiffel tower,
At the wide world in front of me, simply so simple,
Longing for lovers to come and cherish the moments it has to offer,
As seconds perforates millions.

The coming down of the tower is coming down to reality,
The reality of people who do not know love,
This is a wish for everyone to visit this aesthetic place,
To spread love; North, East, South and West.

The magical, soft vibes filtering the land of Disney,
Where dreams for all creatures great and small come true,
Where every moment savoured is as sweet as honey,
The land that brings love, harmony and peace in clear view.

Shamim Razaq

To Keats

The warm seasons of mist
Still live today. The mellow
Fruitfulness season
Sends waves of rhythm.

The melancholy
Fit still falls, falls and falls.
And the world is still
Purified by the glowing,
And shimmering moon.

The spicy colours
of burnt chips of wood
still sends shafts of warmness
In the autumn air.

But Autumn is
Beginning to settle
And bring the freeze,
With the thorns and evergreens,
Still, something is glowing inside.

The Lotus Flower

Every snowdrop
Finally melts and
Things begin to resolve,
And the seasons change.

The buds begin to bud,
Flowers begin to fill the air,
And the warm season comes
All over again, the leaves fall,
Rustling and dancing in the breeze.

They dance in silhouettes,
Like profiled patterns,
Putting words on paper, yet again,
These will soon rest on
The bookshelf, the writers den.

Shamim Razaq

Save The Boy Who Cried Alpha Wolf

In a faraway forest,
Where the sweet berries grow,
Lives an alpha wolf so loyal,
With the brightest star like eyes,
And glowing moon like face.

With fur so whitely rare and a nature so subtle,
He ignites with his soft wild eyes,
With a flame of security, reality and inner stability,
As he teaches humanity to do justice to modesty.

He moves with his fearless eyes
Mesmerising, shaking from inside,
So sleek, so strong is he and so unique,
With colours of peace and unity.

The Lotus Flower

He brings back life,
Wise as a wolf yet mysterious as the moon,
As his vision is in sync with the moon,
Watching so intensely, he draws in,
Causing waves of sentiments to move.

In a faraway corner, in the depth of his heart,
There is a boy who wants to cry wolf,
With casement clear eyes, so deep,
His manly nature has been misunderstood,
For the big bad wolf in fairy tales,
As he fights, to bring the best out of his breast.

Shamim Razaq

Life in seasons

The sparkly, slithery sand,
Immersed with the silvery rays
Like wildflowers powdered over land
This will echo idyllic moments in coming days.

In the frothy watery waves,
The footstep will fade away,
The smooth cells of sand it was,
Will welcome another as it waits.

With silver, smooth-tongued breeze,
The reflection will speak misty days,
Fresh, fleeting flashes will tease,
Like rough rusty autumn leaves.

In the long stinging freeze,
The land will be distilled,
From the runny liquid breeze
to wintery ice drops, chilled.

Unbreakable

Lustrous face, shell like, emitting light
Innocently shines bright.
Rises to the surface by volcanic eruptions,
In high temperatures and pressure conditions,
With intrinsic moral traditions.

A symbol of integrating eternity,
Where atoms are united covalently,
Unequal to any other bond.

But locked in someone's trinket box,
Somewhere in a dark isolated spot-
Crying the suffering it has endured.

But its moment will come to shine-
With its magical mystic powers,
In brilliance and in its ocular strength.

Its captured colours of rainbow will rise high,
Shining bright than any other gem,
There will be no limit, reaching beyond the sky.

Shamim Razaq

I Still Write Butterfly

Each day my thoughts violet, green and indigo
Am going beyond the life of my aviary,
With hollow airwaves busk, tailwind chiming through the open window,
Ringing religious ears I sit tailored writing exploring the human dome,
To reclaim my Muslim heritage as my own,
To capture the vibrations of my celestial ancestral soil,
Calling me to come and grow in its fruitful land,
In pensive mood and paper boat stream vision,
The future children ask to give them a helping hand,
I offer you my breathing book words,
That will provide the momentum for growth,
To offer a helping hand to offer some hope,
Along the wonderland circuit life of Islamic oath,
Prey to inner clashes of rainstorms I still sit and write butterfly.

Phoenix

(7th March 2013)

The reckoning of lovers blessed,
Holds secrets to the phoenix nest,
With beauty so timely rare,
Rises with romantic quill and feathers fair.

The landscaped skies,
The diamond tinted eyes,
Rosary prayers, tasbeeh beads,
Rosemary scent and apple seeds:

Sacred recitations, heartfelt words,
In sync with Allah (swt) blessed birds,
The warm breeze waves,
Blessed by angels – souls saved.

Breaths of grief; breaths of spring,
Illuminated by spreaded wings,
Past death; past cries forever disguised,
With rainbow arc – lovers immortalised.

Shamim Razaq

World of Prosody

(19th March 2013)

A saved life with a true smile is
Better than a bitter death,
Breaths of love are purer than diseased breath,
With starlit dreams and moonlight hope,
The hermit in me conceives a star shining bright.
With incite vibes, so cosmic, so white,
I watch in awe at heavens delight,
So sacred so full of life and love,
Away from devils cursed love,
I sit and smile thanking Allah (swt) and his dove,
For purifying my soul and reuniting me,
With Quranic verses that orbit centuries in me
Holding onto Quran words in my heart,
Spreading peace, love, true art—just playing my part,
Gathering goodness from natures vibes,
With love filled lids refined goodness,
With droplet tears,
As love for generations to come,
Let us live for eternity blossoming all parts of humanity.

As angels ascend on believers.
Devils descend on sinners,
Let us reclaim the genius spirit of guardian angels,
Blessed with squill like falling flakes of snow,
From heavens above,
Blessed children with angelic looks,
Making way for Allahs call,
As I send my children musical beats of the final drum,
To light their hearts,
To sing the rhythm of eternity,
To live beyond earthly contradictions-

My children—I walk within your bittersweet shadow,
Every beat of every abstemious step,
Containing your olive lit pupil candle –
'Let them wander in olive blessed green land,
Let them grow within mother natures blessed hand,
Let the love, grow, laugh, play a strong heart.'

The scattered departed clouds,
Still look close from land
Diffusing, flowing, orbiting and pouring from blessed sky—
The root based mountain point,
The snowstruck sun,
The sun based earth,
The sundering voices aloud uniting sundial time,
In my spiritual mind,
With heightened awareness
The craziness of lovers eyes,
Turns dreams to temporary phoenix ashes,
As the lover wanders through deserted alleys,
In search of soul and twin heartbeat,
Turning heard but still unheard voices inside out,
And outside in,
Cutting the cry of a mothers womb along the way,
Let the mother cry her loudest cry yet,
Temporarily disabling the sacred visions,
Still-
They rise true to phoenix nature,
With renewed heartbeat visions,
To save the divine love based soul,
As the flicker of light,
Continues to shine upwards,

My visions continuously move forward,
My lost footsteps wandering,
Across bridges with visions,
With yesterdays golden crescent moon,
Still –
I dream of dreams
To make way,
In my world of prospected prosody.

Shamim Razaq

Possibilities of Algorhythm

The cameo layers of the fuschia tinted burgundy rose:
Dances –
Protected by spirited resonating sepals,
To the rhythms of immortal love,
Singing amongst the summers light breeze,
With children of all colours humming along dancing bees,
With laughing vibes fusing the beamlight of the halo sun,
Growing with flowing semilunar valves,
In crescent times of fine art celestial epiphany visionary dreams,
Depreciating distorted ambiguities and impassive disabilities,
Appreciating Allah (swt) secured starred energies,
With religious catechism in growing analogies,
Overcoming childhood adversities,
To grow, to blossom in peak time of heartbeat rhythm,
Understanding fundamentals of Algebraic algorhythm,
Blessed with flakes of early spring snow—
Wondering—the endless possibilities of Almighty Allah (swt) show.

A Spectrum of Altruism in Autobiographical Autism

The summer rainbow carries visions of autopsy Autism life,
Where her childhood traumas magnetised the future brainchild,
With eternal power of intelligent life versus the temporary power of a single death,
Moves to extreme poles of the divine dome playing hide and seek with black breath,
Frightening the daylights of a child blessed: voices distorted, taste buds haunted,
With double retina eyes so reserved and emotions so detached—
What is it that she didn't understand?

The ghostly ashen white blood cell lines that her finger writes,
On nights that veiled walls that distorted her visions in daylight,
If only walls could speak the hidden fears of autopsy autism,
The world would make sense of autobiographical altruism in autism,
When the star lighted white gold hair,
Angelic hands held ghostly candlelight,
In blessed Ramadan –
That cameo strengthened the spiritual child with immuned light,
She wanted to run to mother to share her insight
But covered her visions in duvet weak but tight.

Still the sacred scarred degrees of all senses in sight
Brings real life paintings to new heights,
With colours that speak the rhythm of life,
After the brainstorm that brings language to life,
The senses enlightened pentagram starry sight,
Communicating with Allah (swt) with heartfelt soul,
Behind daily visions of white salah –
Violet and gold, a fusion of unity connecting humanity,
Leaves her with a soul smile—so different
Yet so real with the ring of halo light she knows how to heal,
With Prophet Muhammad (pbuh) restoring religion based soul she is guided to love,
To live a life of colour and peace,
In this world that unites healing hearts with healing hands.

As the soul based love came as guiding faith
In daily peaks of pillared salah,
Turning to Allah (swt) grateful for uniting souls that built sandcastles –
Dreams were made,
The red and gold bride sang soprano diamond notes
In castle with particles of alabaster dust,
Her visions carried her forward in time to the language of love,
Wrapped with the crescent time of Islam
Directed to starry stars of the night,
And clusters of olive tree blessed eyes with leaves,
Thanking Allah (swt) for the equinox of creed based earthly reality.